OKLAHOMA
TRAIL RIDE

SHERRY MOSS WALRAVEN

PROISLE PUBLISHING

© COPYRIGHT 2024 BY SHERRY MOSS WALRAVEN

ISBN: 978-1-963735-21-5 (Paperback)
978-1-963735-22-2 (E-book)

All rights reserved. No part of this book may be reproduced or transmitted in any form or by any means, electronic or mechanical, including photocopying, recording, or by any information storage and retrieval system, without permission in writing from the copyright owner.

The views expressed in this work are solely those of the author and do not necessarily reflect the views of the publisher, and the publisher disclaims any responsibility for them.

To order additional copies of this book, contact:

Proisle Publishing Services LLC
39-67 58th Street, 1st floor
Woodside, NY 11377, USA
Phone: (+1 646-480-0129)
info@proislepublishing.com

The more that you read, the more things you will know. The more that you learn, the more places you'll go."

Dr. Seuss

"I have no greater joy than to hear that my children walk in truth."

3 John 1:4

Table of Contents

- Chapter One 1
- Chapter Two 4
- Chapter Three 7
- Chapter Four 11
- Chapter Five 17
- Chapter Six 22
- Chapter Seven 28
- Chapter Eight 31
- Chapter Nine 34
- Chapter Ten 39
- Chapter Eleven 43
- Chapter Twelve 45
- Chapter Thirteen 47
- Chapter Fourteen 50
- Chapter Fifteen 53
- Chapter Sixteen 55
- Chapter Seventeen 58
- Chapter Eighteen 61
- Chapter Nineteen 63
- Chapter Twenty 66
- Chapter Twenty-One 68
- Chapter Twenty-Two 70
- Chapter Twenty-Three 72
- Chapter Twenty-Four 75
- Chapter Twenty-Five 77
- Chapter Twenty-Six 80
- Chapter Twenty-Seven 83

CHAPTER TWENTY-EIGHT 86
CHAPTER TWENTY-NINE 88
CHAPTER THIRTY 92
CHAPTER THIRTY-ONE 94
CHAPTER THIRTY-TWO 96
CHAPTER THIRTY-THREE 101
CHAPTER THIRTY-FOUR 104
CHAPTER THIRTY-FIVE 106
CHAPTER THIRTY-SIX 109
CHAPTER THIRTY-SEVEN 111
CHAPTER THIRTY-EIGHT 113
CHAPTER THIRTY-NINE 116
CHAPTER FORTY 119
CHAPTER FORTY-ONE 123
CHAPTER FORTY-TWO 127
CHAPTER FORTY-THREE 130
EPILOGUE 132

CHAPTER ONE

The Oklahoma summer sun was shining brightly, as a sweet lady called, Jayne, ran to the big red barn with good news for her hard-working husband. He stopped brushing his favorite steed to watch his wife bend over to such a huge degree, so she could retrieve her breath. He couldn't imagine what could have made her this happy, but it always made him happy to see his wife happy.

"Okay, little lady, tell me why you are so giggly," the tickled husband asked with a slight curiosity. It wasn't usual for her to get this way early in the morning. This morning she is not just happy, but jumping up and down happy. Buzz figured it must be good.

"Buzz, you won't believe it. I got a phone call from Olive. She asked if the cousins could come for their visit in two weeks," Jayne could barely wait to see her new friends. Buzz and Buxton came home from a hunting trip in Arkansas telling her about a group of girl cousins they had met. Not long ago, she met them in person and couldn't believe how they made fast friends with the girls. She could hardly wait to see everyone.

"I hope you told them it was okay," Buzz laughed, but he was also exhilarated. He wasn't to the degree his wife was by the looks of her jumping up and down. He wasn't really a jumper, but he was excited just the same that the girls were coming. Buzz thought he better call his brother,

Buxton, because he was in Arkansas with Buzz where they met the cousins.

Jayne knew she had a lot to do before their guests arrived. "I have so much to do and only two weeks to accomplish it all. I need to clean out the bunkhouse and plan everything," Jayne wanted to get started as soon as possible. It goes without saying that Jayne's brain was on fire over her visitors. She couldn't wait to see them. They were more like sisters with the girls.

Buzz knew his wife would get everything done and done very well. That was just in her nature. He began thinking about the first time he met these crazy ladies. Buxton, his brother, and he went on a hunting trip to Arkansas last year. He was amazed at the girls' talent to take care of themselves. Buxton was just as amazed as Buzz was with the ladies who had guns and knew how to use them.

Jayne and Buzz went to Olive's house when all the cousins were there together, and they invited them to come for a visit. He didn't think they would come but was glad they were. He knew, without a doubt, they all would make this a visit to remember. He couldn't wait to call his brother with the good news. He knew he would be excited as much as Jayne was about this visit. They never thought about them really coming, but they were happy they did make the trip.

Buzz knew he needed to call his brother about this visit the ladies were making out here. Buzz picked up his phone and put in Buxton's number. After Buxton heard the news Buzz told him, he was exhilarated about what he just heard. "You are kidding me, right?" He couldn't wait to see the girls. They were so much fun to be around, and Jayne couldn't wait to have fun with these ladies. Every now and then, a person needs to laugh and have fun.

"Yes, they are really coming and will be here in two weeks. If you have time, you can come help me clean up a few things around the ranch," Buzz laughed at his brother's eagerness. "You will need to help me pick out the horses for the ladies to ride." They knew they could ride, but they would still pick out a horse to match the person.

"Great. See you then. You need to stay for supper when you get here," Buzz knew his brother didn't get many home-cooked meals, since his wife decided she didn't like ranch life, and she ran away. He doesn't have a clue where she could be, but he can't let himself get in a bad way. If his wife doesn't want to be here, then he will need to learn to live here alone. Who knows what may happen? The right girl may be closer than he thinks.

"Sounds good to me," Buxton was smiling as he hung up his phone from his brother. He thought the girls coming would be a good thing for him. They all make him laugh, and that is exactly what he needs right now. I shouldn't have let myself get in this state to start with. If my wife doesn't want to be here, then I will need to learn to live here alone all by myself. He certainly wasn't going to live in a big city like his wife wanted him to do.

CHAPTER TWO

The enchanting ladies talked and laughed as they stored their luggage in Callie's big red van with the white stripe. The cousins decided they would all meet and ride together to see Buzz, Jayne, and Buxton in Oklahoma. They couldn't wait to see them and have some fun. They were looking forward to the scenery along the way to Oklahoma. After looking around, they decided it was beautiful here in Oklahoma.

"There's a taxi coming up the driveway," smiled Olivia. She wondered who it could be until she noticed a tall woman inside. They knew, without a doubt, it had to be their friend from Texas. She was the tallest lady they had ever seen before.

The stimulating cousins all stopped what they were doing and watched Tinker open the taxi door, and instantly ran to meet them. What surprised the cousins more was that Tinker had her trusty ball bat in her hands. After the greetings and hugs, nine smiling ladies hurdled out of Callie's van to begin their next adventure in Oklahoma with good friends. Things were looking up.

"How are things in Texas, Tinker?" Jas asked, with a huge grin. Jas knew strange things often happen around Tinker, but she also knew Tinker is a good one to have on your side when needed. She could swing a ball bat like Babe Ruth.

"I've been a touch sad. Do you remember the old man who took me to the airport when we were all at Olive's house?" Tinker had tears in her eyes as she gazed at the others. They couldn't think why Tinker would cry. She just wasn't the crying kind of girl.

"We remember you talking about him. What happened?" Grandee asked. She really liked some of Tinker's stories. Grandee remembers her visit to Tinker's cabin when her chickens and pigs came out from under the cabin and chased her all around Tinker's cabin. Good times. It wasn't something she often thought about very much.

"It happened not long after his wife ran away with the old man who owns the Feed and Seed store. Earl was so sad, he just ambled around the farm all day. Last week he was walking around crying, making his eyes all blurry. He walked in his pig pen and his feet slipped right out from under him, and just as pretty as you please, it made him fall down in the slippery mud and poop. He fell face down in a mud puddle that was full of pig feces."

"Oh my, Tinker. Drowning in a puddle in a pig pen is not a good way to go." Alaska said as she was trying not to giggle.

"Falling in the pig pen puddle didn't kill him," Tinker began to giggle. She knew the others were wanting to giggle, so she just started it. "It was sort of funny." Tinker was still giggling.

"Then what killed him?" They all sat with mouths wide open to hear how her friend went to meet his maker. It must be a horrible story.

"After he hosed off all the pig poop, he went to the barn to milk his old fat cow. Her name is Snow White. I always thought it was funny to name a black cow Snow White, but anyway, the cow became restless. She knocked over the milk pail, and then she proceeded to sit on poor old Earl, making him flat as a flitter. That is why he is no longer with us." The girls were trying their best not to laugh, but how could one not laugh?

"How did you get to the airport?" Phoenix asked as soon as she stopped laughing. Phoenix knew Tinker didn't drive.

"I hate to break up this lovely story, but I wanted you to know that we are here at the ranch." Callie was keeping her eye on the GPS. She pulled up in the van right after the Taxi let Tinker out. She is usually observant about her surroundings. The girls thought the GPS said it was thirty miles away, but here they were. Callie was right about being at the ranch. They all jumped out of the van and went to where Tinker was telling their story.

"Wow, just think. We were less than thirty minutes away for some fun and gaiety." They knew Jayne was going to be the best hostess ever. She seemed to be someone who knew how to do everything that needed to be done.

CHAPTER THREE

The jolly ladies spent the last thirty miles talking and laughing about all the adventures they had together while on their vacations. They decided the adventures only made them stronger, or it could be in their bloodline. They found out about their heritage lately that centuries ago their family was Royalty. They laughed and made jokes about it, but it didn't bother them one way or another. That was back in the 1200s.

All the lady cousins were not all the cousins. They just happen to be the girl cousins. Sometimes, a few boy cousins would travel with them, but they couldn't keep up with the active girls. The last time the boys went with them, they were captured by a motorcycle gang who wanted Stone's truck. They were kept in a cave with a live tiger, so they don't go too much anymore. Every time they have been with the girls, something always happens to them, so they usually stay home now. They will go some more, but they said they would be more careful. If they do go, they made the girls promise they were not going to go to a place where they would see a tiger.

All the ladies have had their own share of troubles in their lives, but nothing they couldn't come out of with a lot of determination to fix it. The girls always helped each other. They were a close family.

They had their own personalities, but also had some just alike. They got along well, which made for fun times. Callie and Houston are the oldest and can help plan their trips and activities. The rest of the girls have some of the same personalities. They laugh, plan, and help each other.

Callie usually does all the planning of the trips, after they all agree on where to go. She has that job because she was a teacher and her planning strategy was what she did best, because teachers need to be organized. She could be a bit imperious at times, but no one ever gets mad. They laugh about it, and Callie laughs right along with them. Callie would help anyone who was in trouble and Houston would be right there by her side.

Houston can also organize like Callie, but she can also figure out what needs to be done in bad situations, in which they have had some. Like all the girls, she likes to laugh and have a good time on their annual vacations.

Jas is another one who can think of ways to get themselves out of trouble. She smiles all the time and makes everyone laugh. They truly miss her when she doesn't come with them, but that is rare. She loves to go on their vacations. She wouldn't stay away unless something was terribly wrong at home.

Grandee is known to be the family gigglier. The family all know she got the giggle gene from her mom, who also giggled a great deal. There have been a few times that one of the cousins had to put her hand over Grandee's mouth when it wasn't a good time to giggle, but all in all, she would help anyone if they needed help, just like all the girls would do. The others knew she giggled, at times, but they didn't say anything. They were used to it.

Phoenix lives the farthest away from the others, but she still flies to meet the girls on occasion, and when they are going on one of their annual vacations. She likes her time with the girls, because it helps her get rid of stress from her job. She spends some of her free time from work riding horses. She really knows how to handle villains, and that helps everyone out. They pity the poor soul who gets between her and her iron skillet. Sometimes in a bad situation, she picks up whatever she can find, and usually comes out the winner.

Olive is another one of the cousins who smiles a great deal and loves to have fun and laugh, which they do quite often when they are all together. She was captured on one of their vacations in Missouri, but she never gave up on her cousins rescuing her. She wasn't disappointed, because they found her and came inside the apartment, where she was being kept, with guns and a smile. Olive is another one who smiles a lot and can make them all laugh.

Olivia, like all the girls, comes equipped with the family fun gene, and loves their excursions with her cousins. She didn't call them vacations anymore. She likes to think of them as an adventure they have never had before. Since she is the only nurse in the bunch, she has often had to tend to the wounds of the one that was hurt. It didn't bother her. She was happy to be away from work for a while, after all, she did become a nurse to help people. She is full of life and will often do something that others wouldn't do. She has been known to look over people's fences to see what they were doing.

Alaska is the last of the cousins. It goes with saying, that she likes all the same things as the others do. No one would believe it, but Alaska was taken captive by a British soldier on one of their vacations. Another thing about her is she loves to wear her red high heels everywhere she goes. She has been known to wear her high heels riding a horse and walking in the woods.

One thing they all have in common is their parents, who were close and met together every year. One year, as a joke, they thought it would be fun to name their daughters after cities and states, while the boys would be named after Confederate Generals. That is exactly what they did. After all, they were raised in the South. Some of the cousins shortened their original names to make it easier to say.

CHAPTER FOUR

The cheerful ladies drove along the long driveway to the ranch of Buzz and Jayne. They were not able to contain their joy. They are fun people along with being good people. They couldn't wait until all the fun they were sure to have. They met Buzz and Buxton on a hunting trip, and Buzz was sure his wife would like these gun-toting ladies.

"Wow! What a beautiful home they have," said Olive with a great big smile as she gazed at the pretty stucco sides and heavy-duty double doors. She was so glad to finally arrive at the ranch. She couldn't wait for the fun to begin. All the cousins had met Jayne while they paid a visit to Olive's house one Halloween.

Phoenix had her eye on the huge red barn. The other girls thought Phoenix was probably drooling, now that she was becoming this close to horses. They all smiled at her spellbinding excitement because they were all happy to be there. This would be a good visit for some of the cousins who needed a change away from work, or for whatever was bothering them.

The ladies all were laughing, as they noticed Jayne running out the door toward the van. They all jumped out of the van to meet her. Jayne began hugging all of them at one time. She was laughing because she had been waiting for so long to see the ladies again. Among all the hoopla, she noticed Tinker. Tinker was already there due to riding in a

Taxi. Jayne was amazed when she saw Tinker with her ball bat in her arms. Jayne ran to hug Tinker. She was more than happy to see her new friend. Jayne was the kind of lady that loved everyone. She never said a bad word about anyone. The cousins decided they would help Jayne in the kitchen. She may have to cook extra food.

"Tinker, I am so glad you came. I was hoping you would come with the girls. Now we can have some fun," Jayne said. Her smile seemed to go on forever. Jayne couldn't contain her laughter. She was so happy the gang was all here. Jayne was hoping all the girls would have a great time.

Tinker couldn't believe her good luck to have more friends than she ever had before. She was jubilant to just think about it, "Thank you so much for having me." Jayne walked over to Tinker and gave her a huge hug. Tinker was tickled to have all the girls here. Houston told Jayne that Tinker didn't have many friends until she met the cousins, and now she has plenty. Tinker smiled the entire time she is with the cousins.

Buzz and Buxton came out the front door with mammoth smiles as they noticed the ladies were finally here. The hugging began again as Buzz and Buxton wanted to greet their friends. Buzz and Buxton liked these girls, and he liked having his wife being this happy. It gives her some time to spend with their guests.

"Come inside. We have lunch on the table," Buzz stated. "We figured out when you might arrive here since you let us know where you were the last time you called.

You made good time. We are glad you could get away to visit us. I think we will have a grand ole time. I think everyone will have a good time going on a trail ride and spending the night." It sure was something the cousins had never done before, and they were so excited. Buzz was glad the cousins came. He knew they all like to have fun and laugh.

"So, tell us about the last trip you made," Buxton said. He loved hearing about their holidays, which were often more like adventures than a vacation. The girls called their trip holidays because of all the fun they have. It was true about their vacations. They had some experiences they wished they never had, but everyone always came back in one piece.

"We often get our trips mixed up," Alaska said while eating the delicious meal. "We always have fun no matter where we go. The main thing is the people we meet and the strange things we have done, but we always have fun. Some have been taken, but the cousins could always rescue them."

"Did we tell you about going to the haunted house in Louisiana?" Jas asked. She couldn't remember the last one they went on either. It was such fun.

"We could have done without the snakes and the alligator that chased us back to the house, but it was one of our favorites," Jas really liked that trip. We had fun one night when the owners did a scavenger hunt. It was so much fun.

Buzz glanced at the girls, "I think you did mention it. Alligators and snakes, I believe is what you said, right?"

"Yes, it was right. We also did the zip-lining. Callie was the only one who had ever zip-lined. The man told the girls to do exactly what Callie did. Some got it and some didn't. I remember the man had to push off the ones who were afraid. We also met some older ladies that were hilarious," Houston said with a sneaky smile.

"You got that right. I don't care if I ever see another gator or a snake in my lifetime. Grandee cringes every time someone says anything about a snake. She is terrified of them, so they usually don't mention one of those in front of her. Grandee goes off the deep end just thinking about a snake." Olivia wasn't too fond of snakes either, but she didn't tell the others.

"These ribs and potato salad are delicious," Callie said, as she chowed down the last of her ribs. You would have thought she was a lumberjack, but Jayne likes for people to like her meals. They were sure she was the best cook around.

"When everyone is finished with lunch, Buxton will hook-up the horses to the wagon, and we will take a ride to show you the ranch," Jayne said, while still smiling at her invited guests. They all agreed it was a great idea and couldn't wait to see it all. The guests filled up the wagon, but they couldn't wait to get started. This was another first for them, and they were all loving the ride. Their ranch was beautiful.

"We would love that," Olivia said. "Don't go to any trouble for us. We usually are self-sufficient."

"I can't wait to see everything, especially the horses," Phoenix smiled. She loved to see horses. Everyone in the wagon chuckled at Phoenix for wanting to see the horses.

They all gathered in the antique wagon, with Buzz and Buxton guiding the horses. The girls noticed they were on a long dirt road that wasn't very wide. It made them feel like they were back in time traveling down a trail. The girls were liking everything they were seeing, especially the wagon ride. They imagined themselves in a long gingham dress with a pretty bonnet. That image didn't last too long.

"Over to your right you will see the big pond where the cattle drink their water, and on the left is the pasture where the horses are." They stopped for a while so everyone could look around and take a little walk. Buzz knew the girls had been sitting for a long time to travel all the way from Georgia to Oklahoma for a long time, so he thought they might appreciate the stroll.

Buxton smiled and said, "The little cabin you see up ahead is where our great-grandparents lived long ago. They built it themselves and cut the trees by themselves. It's not used anymore. You can go inside and look around if you want to."

"We would love to go in the cabin." They had already imagined being in a long dress and bonnet, Jas was excited wishing she had on the fake dress and bonnet.

The girls thought that would be a good idea. They stood in amazement while looking around the antique cabin that hadn't been used in many years. There were two old bunkbeds that were almost rotten, a kitchen with two shelves, and an old wash pan, where they apparently washed their dishes. They ambled back to the wagon with smiles on their tired faces. That was great. They loved historic sites. The girls couldn't wait to see it. They didn't think they would like to live like that, but it was so amazing to know people who really did.

"Thank you for showing the cabin to us. It was amazing to see and to think about people really living there," Tinker said. "It made you wonder how they probably cooked over a fire in the fireplace and lots of other things we wouldn't like to do."

Alaska looked at her cousins and said, "I sure couldn't live like this because I couldn't use my hair dryer. My hair won't do anything in the mornings."

Their last stop was the bunkhouse where they would be staying. The girls didn't know what to expect, but what they saw was not what they were expecting. The ten twin beds were all prettied up with beautiful spreads, curtains, and everything was spotless. Thank goodness, they saw a bathroom at the end of the hallway. They couldn't wait to stay in a bunkhouse. It was another thing they had never done before. They knew there would be a few things different, and they would do some things they may never do again. That wasn't going to bother the cousins. They like a good adventure.

Chapter Five

The sleeping ladies, who were enjoying their slumber, began to move around by the strange noise that was loud and shrill. They thought someone had a strange alarm on their phone and wanted everyone to hear the loud alarm.

"What was that horrible noise? Tinker, get your ball bat and make it stop. It sounds like it's a huge monster," cried Grandee, who had never lived in the country.

Tinker smiled as she said, "Before I slay the horrible monster, I need to tell you Buzz and Jayne would not like us killing their rooster."

Grandee began laughing, "You know I'm a city girl. I have never been awakened by a rooster before."

After much laughter, they all began stirring around to meet the day. Callie noticed two of their happy group were missing, "Does anyone know where Olivia and Olive might be? Surely, we have not lost them." It was too early in the trip to lose someone. Normally, that is later in the vacation.

Houston, who was still chuckling over Grandee's friend, the rooster, said, "They were awake early, and you know me, I don't sleep all night. They told me they were going to the house to help Jayne with the preparation of breakfast." They were glad someone is helping prepare a meal for so many of them. Perhaps, they could take turns helping Jayne cook.

"That was sweet of them. They do have a lot more mouths to feed," Jas was still giggling over Grandee's mean old rooster. Jas thought Grandee will get used to waking up to the rooster here at the ranch.

They all went toward the house for their morning meal. Jayne met them with a mammoth smile, as she directed the ladies to the back door, where they noticed a large table on the beautiful, tiled patio. The best part of eating out there was the alluring scenery. The cousins loved this place. They thought they could live like this. "This is the way to have breakfast first thing in the morning, watching the goodness that God made" Olive smiled.

Breakfast was more of a feast rather than a simple morning meal. With stomachs filled, they sat talking and having fun. Jayne was thrilled the girls all came to visit. She was hoping they would come when Buzz told her he had invited them to come any time. He didn't think they would really come, but he was so glad they did.

"Where are Buzz and Buxton this morning?" Alaska asked while smiling when she noticed Jayne looking at her red high heels Alaska was wearing. Maybe she couldn't believe someone would wear high heels on a ranch, but it brought about a sweet smile. "I have some boots if you don't want to wear the high heels. They are pretty, but not enough to wear on a ranch." Jayne offered, but she didn't know what Alaska would do.

Jayne looked at the ladies with a wide smile, "They are at the pit overseeing the meat for our BBQ Barn Dance tonight. We will invite a few of our friends and neighbors.

You will love them. They all are good people." The girls liked meeting new people. It was like a hobby for them. The girls loved meeting new people, so they were excited to go to the barn dance tonight.

"That sounds like fun," Callie said while smiling. She was a hyper girl, who loved to dance. Her cousins sometimes think that she gets excited over everything, but the others do, too. The other cousins knew Callie was hyper, but they loved to watch her dance.

Houston, who was excited about the BBQ and the Barn Dance, told Jayne to let them help set up the barn, and anything else that needs doing. Houston told Jayne she would be able to help set up everything.

"Good idea," Jayne said. "Let's go to the barn and I'll tell you what we usually do, and feel free to give me any ideas you may have." "Okay, ladies, let's go see what we can get into. To the barn we go." Jayne laughed all the way to the barn. She was more excited than all the others.

They finished the barn in record time. Jayne suggested lunch, so they went to eat the lunch Jayne had prepared for them. They sat at the outside table again. The sub sandwiches and pasta salad were just what they needed after preparing the barn for the festivities that were going on tonight. The lunch was delicious, and everyone seemed to be happy.

"Can we help with the preparing of the food for tonight?" Olive asked as she threw out her signature sweet smile that was bigger than the moon.

"I would be more than glad to help you with the food for tonight," Jas offered to help, also.

"Buzz and Buxton will take care of the BBQ. I have already finished the potato salad. It's in the fridge. I mixed up some homemade rolls, but they need to be rolled out and put on pans to bake. Some of you can make the dessert that I haven't made yet. The recipe is on the counter. Thank you so much for your help." Jayne never had so much fun while cooking. The girls were singing and dancing the entire time in the huge kitchen. "Sometimes we dance and sing while cooking. We are sure it makes the food happy," Callie says. She was sure it was good for the food.

Tinker had never seen anything like what the ladies, who were helping in the kitchen, were doing. It made her laugh, so she started dancing, also. Tinker is so tall, she danced in an awkward way, but they loved to see her happy. "You go, Tinker. Good job,"

"Thanks, ladies." Tinker couldn't think she had ever danced while preparing a meal.

Before they knew it, the time had come to take the food to the barn, because it wasn't long before the guests would start arriving. The girls could hardly wait for the festivities to begin. They were so glad they finally decided to come for a visit.

All the guests at the Barn Dance had a wonderful time. The friends and neighbors of Buzz and Jayne loved the lady guests, and the ladies loved the friends and neighbors. Everyone was filled with joyful feeling as they went to their homes—or their bunkhouse, in the case of the nine elated ladies.

Tinker, who had never been to a Barn Dance before, was shooting out a smile that could brighten a large room. Men really asked her to dance. The cousins looked at her with happy smiles to see her so excited. The cousins really liked seeing Tinker so happy. She thought no one would ask her to dance, because she was so tall, but it didn't bother anyone. There were quite a few tall cowboys there. The girls liked seeing Tinker that happy. It made all her friends break out with large smiles. Tinker never had so much fun before all at one time.

Chapter Six

As the hungry ladies made their way to the house for breakfast on another beautiful day, they began talking about the great weather they had while here. It made the ladies think everything would be harmless on their trail ride, they couldn't wait to get this party started.

At the breakfast table, there was excitement in the air. They had a great time the night before at the Barn Dance and couldn't wait to get their day started today. The happy gaggle of women were so glad they came to have some fun. It wasn't every day they got together with each other.

"What are we doing today?" Jas asked, who couldn't wait to see what was in store for them today. She was thinking this may be a lot of fun. She loved riding horses, and the barn dance was another thing she thought was great. This was starting to become one of her favorite holidays.

Buzz smiled at the people around the table, "We need to get everything ready for the trail ride. We are taking one of our small wagons for our personal things, along with our food and any other things we need to take. We will take a big wagon with huge mattresses in it for the ladies to sleep on. If you want to sleep in a sleeping bag by the fire, you may, but I know my wife won't sleep on the ground, so whoever wants to sleep in the wagon, that's okay." Some of the girls were thankful for the mattresses.

"I will sleep on the ground by the fire," Phoenix said, who had gone camping before and slept on the ground in her sleeping bag. She enjoyed being by the fire, and she loves horses. This was a great vacation for her.

"I will also sleep on the ground," Tinker said with a huge smile. The girls know how Tinker wants to take care of them, and they admired her for it. It made the others feel safe with Tinker being their bodyguard. Before meeting Tinker when they went to a Dude Ranch in Texas, they found out she didn't have many friends. They told her when they left the Dude Ranch that she was now their friend. The girls taught her some things, but most of all she was their friend. Now she had eight friends.

That may have come from living far away from civilization in a cabin. The cousins really liked Tinker and will always be her friend. They knew she was a sensitive and loyal friend for life.

"Great, we have plenty of sleeping bags," Buxton said. He was enjoying having the ladies here. He thought they were fun to be around, plus it gets his bad thoughts out of his mind about his wife who left him. The girls glanced at Buxton and felt sorry about his wife, but they saw his smile and knew he was okay. The cousins would pray for Buxton to get a nice girlfriend.

Buzz began shooting out orders. "Four of the ladies will help Jayne collect the food and other things they will need for cooking while camping. The rest of the ladies will load sleeping bags, lanterns, etc. Buxton and I will load hay for the horses, and barrels of water. After everything is loaded on the wagons, we put them in the barn."

Buxton smiled at the girls, "When the wagons are finished and put in the barn, we will be giving you a horse. You need to be familiar with your horse before riding a long way tomorrow, so we will all go riding for a while today. It will be an easy ride today, and you will get to see more of the country." The girls all agreed to see more of the countryside.

Buzz looked at the ladies, "We will have lunch, and after we finish, we ride. I think you ladies will enjoy the ride."

"Buck has saddled-up the horses we will be riding. Before we get on our horses, I need to know if you ladies brought your pistols with you," Buzz had no doubts they brought them, and he knew that, for sure. He saw on his hunting trip what the girls could do.

As soon as Buzz asked that question about them having their guns, eight pistols were raised up high in the air, and Tinker, who had her ball bat up in the air too.

Buzz, Jayne, Buck, and Buxton were laughing, "Wow!" Jayne said. "Did you boys see that?" Jayne was amazed, to say the least.

"Yes, ma'am. That would have been hard to miss," laughed Buck, who helped around the ranch. The nine ladies, who came for a visit, couldn't wait to get this trail ride started. Buck was beginning to really like these ladies.

Oklahoma Trail Ride

The girls' noticed Buck was staring at Phoenix. They saw the wink that was sent to Phoenix from those large blue eyes of Buck's.

Buzz, Buxton, Jayne, and Buck walked out of the barn leading their horses, "Don't worry. All our horses are tame. We have people come here to ride occasionally, and no one has ever had a problem with them. We figured you ladies know what you're doing."

"Come retrieve your horse when I call your name," Buzz smiled, who was elated the girls were here. He knew they all knew how to ride, because they told him about going to a dude ranch on one of their vacations.

"Grandee, come meet Tulip. Don't worry about her. She is a sweetheart," Buxton smiled wondering if Tulip would keep up with the rest of the horses. She is a bit old.

"What a sweet name. I think Tulip and I will be good friends." Grandee smiled at the others. That made Grandee less nervous to know she was going to get a good horse while rubbing her horse's neck.

Jayne called Alaska up to get Peanut. "Peanut got her name when we saw her munching on a bag of peanuts." Alaska liked peanuts too, so she was okay.

"Olivia, come pick up Buttercup," Buzz smiled. Olivia didn't think a horse named Buttercup could be anything but good. Olivia smiled as she got on her horse. It had been a while, but she knew she would be okay. She had been through things worse than mounting a horse called Buttercup.

"Olive, come meet Baby Doll," Jayne assured Olive that Baby Doll was a good ride and a sweetheart. She wouldn't step on a bug. Olive was happy she had a good horse. Sometimes they make her a little nervous, but she felt good about this one. They trusted Buzz and Buxton to give them a good tame horse.

"Jas, you have Sadie. She is gentle as a baby." Jas liked that and couldn't wait to get started on their ride as Buck helped her in the saddle.

"Houston, you may come pick up Ginger," Buzz handed Houston the reins. "She's a good horse." That comment about her horse being a good one made her happy.

"Phoenix, meet Firecracker," Buck handed over the horse to Phoenix with a wink. Phoenix smiled at Buck and thanked him. Buzz knew Phoenix rode more than the others, so she would most likely not have a problem with Firecracker. She liked a little spirit in her horses.

"Callie, come pick up Rosie. If she likes you, Rosie will be your friend forever." Jayne smiled as she handed over the horse. Callie patted Rosie and began talking to her because she wanted Rosie to like her.

Tinker walked up to Buxton, where he was holding on to Precious. "Ah! That is such a sweet name." Tinker smiled as she looked at everyone. She was having fun. She figured you couldn't go wrong with a horse named Precious.

Buzz looked at his guests and said, "Saddle-up ladies. Jayne and I will be in the lead, while Buxton and

Buck will bring up the rear." They were glad to see they wouldn't be alone.

"I see you have your pistols with you. Good. Every now and then, we may see a copperhead." Buzz wanted to make sure they had no surprises. It was better to let them know up front what they might see, especially Grandee, who was scared silly of snakes.

Grandee almost fell off her horse. They laughed at her, but she didn't care. She just laughs along with them. She knew they didn't mean it in a mean way, because they all knew how much she despises snakes. They could just see her now shooting at everything that moved. She didn't really shoot much, because she didn't like guns. She preferred her whip, and she was getting better with it every day.

The short ride today was a good one. Two hours later, they turned around to go back toward Buzz's barn. After they returned, they all went to Jayne's favorite restaurant for dinner. The food was delicious, and everyone was full.

After dinner, everyone went to bed because they had to rise early to eat breakfast, so they could leave early for their overnight trail ride. The ladies could hardly contain their excitement. They had ridden horses, but never have stayed overnight before outside in the dark. The girls were excited because they knew the others would take care of them.

Chapter Seven

After awaking to the strange sounds of a rooster, the ladies began rising from their bunks. They noticed the sun was shining brightly making them all eager to begin their day. The rooster didn't make a loud noise as he did the first time. The rooster was more subdued.

They started walking to the outdoor patio that had a floor of beautiful tiles. The table where they were eating, must be ten feet long. They were glad for the bright day so they could enjoy the view.

Olivia and Olive started bringing out dishes of aromatic foods. Jayne brought out the large coffee pot. After eating a hardy breakfast, everyone started to saunter toward the large red barn laughing while telling Jayne about what woke them up this morning.

The girls saw their horses tied up in the barn. Buck, Buzz, and Buxton came out with all the horses. They mounted their horse while the men bought the wagons out of the barn filled with what was needed to spend the night outside. They were excited, but some were somewhat leery of the adventure.

The men, who were driving the wagons, slowed down as they parked the wagons under large shade trees. The shade felt better than the blaring sun.

"Jayne, do you do this often?" Alaska asked with a smile. *No one will ever make me do this very often.*

"We do it three or four times a year. We have families come to do this every year. They love the adventure they have when they come with their three teenage boys."

"Wow! This is why Jayne is so organized and knows exactly what to do for all tasks. They were glad they had somebody to take care of things.

"She is a wonder, for sure. I don't know what I would do without her," Buzz smiled at his beautiful wife.

Jayne began setting up a small table where she set out sandwiches, small bags of chips, homemade cookies and bottles of water.

"Lunch is served ladies and gentlemen," Jayne said sweetly as she looked at the girls and her husband, who gave her a big wink.

Everyone was thankful for the lunch. The ones who were finished began talking and laughing about some of the cousin's adventures. They often like to tell about some of their adventures while on vacation.

Phoenix was getting antsy to get on Firecracker. She told the others she was going to take a small ride before going farther.

The others watched as Firecracker saw a small pond and began running toward the water. He ran straight into the water and bucked Phoenix off in the cool water.

Everyone began laughing as Phoenix started to come out of the water with drips of the pond running down her face, hair, and body. Phoenix was laughing more than everybody else. She wasn't hurt at all. She thought it was fun. Thank goodness she brought another set of clothes to change into. She didn't think she would need them, but she was glad she brought them now that she was soaking wet when the horse bucked her off.

Chapter Eight

The happy campers finally stopped for the night. Supper would be cooked over an opened fire. They had some left-over ham, pasta, and biscuits Jayne made in an iron skillet. The girls were amazed at how good everything was. This was an amazing experience they had never had before, and they were loving every minute of it while taking it all and putting the memories inside their heads.

Buzz told the girls to unsaddle their horses and tie them to a tree for the night. Buxton showed them the right way to tie their horses, and where to put the saddles for the night. They were all ecstatic about sleeping under the stars.

"Hey girls, look up at the sky at all the stars," Jas kept looking up for a while. She didn't know if she would be able to sleep or not, but she was loving the view of the star-lit sky. She was so glad they came. Everything they had done so far, has been great.

"You're right, Jas. They are beautiful. This is great out here," Alaska told the others. Finally, Alaska has taken off her high heels. She decided to lay back down and enjoy the view.

"What exactly are we doing tomorrow?" Olivia wanted to know. She was loving this trip so far. It had been quite a while since she had been on a horse, but she thought she did good with her horse, and looked forward to another day of fun.

"There is an old-timey country store that we think you would like to see. It has some different kinds of things in it. Everyone we take there really like it," Jayne smiled as she looked at the girls. Jayne liked taking people to the store.

Jayne, Olive, Alaska, Grandee, and Houston said they would be going to the store. They couldn't wait for their next adventure. They didn't know if they had ever been in an old-timey store or not, and the girls could barely wait to see what they had in the old antique store.

Buzz told the ones who were not going to the store would be going to see a cave. Some people call it a magic cave. They didn't know what kind of magic he was talking about, but they liked that it was a different experience. The girls were excited about going in the cave, especially when he said it was a magic cave.

"Wow! That should be a good experience," Jas said with a mammoth smile. Jas smiles all the time at everyone she meets. She couldn't even imagine what a magic cave would look like. Maybe, it has a wishing well, or maybe a pond where you throw in coins. This should be fun.

Callie, Tinker, Phoenix, Olivia, and of course, Jas will be going to the magic cave. Let us know what you think is magical about the cave. Phoenix was thinking it was just something to say to get people to go to the cave, but she would be glad to go with her cousins to see the cave.

The girls, except for the ones who were going to sleep on the ground by the fire, were putting their blankets and pillows on their mattresses, so they could get a good night's sleep. They couldn't wait until morning. Some of the girls had never slept under the stars before, but being the good sports they are, they would do it and will love the experience.

The ladies, who were sleeping by the fire, already had their sleeping bags down on the hard ground. The ones on the ground and the ones on the mattresses could hear the sparks of the fire in the quietness of the night, and they were loving it. "This trip has already been great. We can't wait to have more adventures."

CHAPTER NINE

Birds were singing their bird songs as the sleepy group rose from their slumber while the men were preparing a breakfast of eggs and bacon along with a huge pot of coffee. After a great breakfast, they would be starting their adventure in a cave or a store.

Breakfast was over when they heard Buzz giving directions. "Everyone, start saddling up. Buck and Buxton will help you with that." They started putting on the saddles of the ladies who were riding to the store first. The girls going to the store didn't know what to expect at the store, but they couldn't wait to find out.

Jayne and Buzz were busy washing the pans so they could pack them for the trip back to the house. The girls thought Jayne and Buzz were great people. They did this for people often, so they were proficient in what they did.

Finally, the ones going to the cave mounted their horses. Buzz showed them the way to go to the cave. He told them it wasn't too far away, and it will be easy to find. He told them "there's a good place to tie your horses. Have fun, girls."

"Ladies, be watchful. The radio said a storm was coming in," Jayne says in a sweet voice.

"Thanks Jayne. We can't wait for what we may see in the cave. I'm sure we will like it," Jas said with a smile.

Jayne looked at the smiling girls, "Have fun, girls."

The cave girls couldn't wait to go to a place that is supposed to be a magic cave. Maybe, they have put a clown in there to make people think it is a magic cave.

"Okay, we will be okay. We will wait out the storm in the cave. Don't worry about us," Tinker said with a large smile. She was loving this vacation. She has never been this far from home, or ever had this much fun before all at one time. Tinker lives in a cabin in an isolated place. The cousins call her often, so she will have someone to talk to.

"Thank you, Tinker. We know we can count on you for protection," Callie commented. "You are always looking out for us. We remember when you came to Olive's house to see if we were alright on Halloween. No one has ever gone out of their way to do that for us. Tinker, you will always be our friend."

After tying the horses, the excited ladies finally realized they made it to the cave Buzz told them about. They didn't expect what they saw when they stepped into the cave. There was a couple of old-timey lanterns. At least, they will have light and warmth. They also saw where someone had a campfire. They felt safe in there. "Jayne said a storm is coming so the cave should keep us warm."

They were shocked when they saw a young man who was wearing a funny hat. He had a gun in a holster sitting on his back hip. No one said a word about what they were seeing. No one didn't know what to say. Jas looked at the other girls, "Maybe, it's a hologram so people will think it is a real person."

The ladies heard a noise over in another corner of the cave. They all raised their eyebrows and had mouths open as they gazed on two Indian Chiefs complete with headdresses made of feathers, moccasins on their feet, and what looked like an outfit made from deerskin. They sat side by side with their arms crossed over their chests. The funniest thing was the silly grins on their faces. They all thought it wasn't too scary since they had those silly expressions on their on their tired faces.

One of the Chiefs started talking, "Why you here?" "He crazy. Don't look at him. He ugly," Chief number one said.

Chief number two said, "Women should wear dress —need to wear dress."

"He crazy. Pay no attention to him," Number one says.

The girls laughed at the two Indians arguing with each other. Jas looked at everyone in the cave. She asked the man what his name was. "My name is William H. Bonney, Ma'am, and I sure think you are pretty," Mr. Bonney said as he gazed at Jas.

"Wow! Billy the Kid." Jas was excited as she gazed at Billy. She was beginning to think she was dreaming, or the Sandman had done something to their brain.

Phoenix slowly walked toward the mouth of the cave. She quickly came back inside the cave. She thought they were in another universe.

"Why you go out?" Chief number one said while shaking his head making his feathers shake as they fell all around the other Chief's feet.

"I'm sorry. I just needed some fresh air," Phoenix gave a sneaky smile. It is her signature smile. Phoenix couldn't believe all that was happening around her.

"She touched in head? Raining out there," Chief number two explained. All the girls were giggling as they listened to the banter going back and forth between the two Indians.

That is when the eight people in the cave all heard the rolling thunder. The horses were becoming restless, so they decided they would bring the horses in the cave. The girls along with Billy the Kid, and two arguing Indian Chiefs ran out to get horses. If they don't get the horses, they might run away, and the girls didn't like the idea of walking all the way back.

While everyone was trying to calm their horses, something happened they couldn't explain. The sharp strike of lightening was heard. Instantly, there was a soft white light like a thick cloud in the sky going on inside the cave. That made the ladies a touch nervous. They didn't have a clue what the white cloud was all about.

When the storm was over the Indians, the girls, and Billy the Kid all went out of the dark cave. They all looked around but didn't recognize the area. What they saw looked like an old Western Town complete with a saloon, a Doctor Office, Post Office, and a Bank with the name of Missouri Bank.

"What do we do now?" Callie said in a confused voice. They were pretty sure they were not there to rob a bank.

Chapter Ten

The girls, who went to the Country Store, were looking at everything in the store. They saw some different kinds of things. There were saddles to teacups and fried apple pies. They were glad they came. They kept walking around. They had T-shirts with Oklahoma on the front. The girls thought they would buy one for themselves, and they would buy one for the other girls who went to the cave.

Buzz told them to return at the camp site when they finished. Buzz, Buxton, Buck, and Jayne were sitting in the wagon with the mattress. They noticed they had everything packed up and ready to go. The girls thought they had this whole thing organized.

They were beginning to worry about the ones who went to see the cave. They didn't think they would see too much in the cave, and it worried Jayne because she had been there and knew there wasn't much to see. She was wondering why they were so late returning. She was hoping no one was hurt. If Jayne knew what was really going on in the cave, she would be surprised.

Buzz, Buxton, and Buck jumped on their horses and headed toward the cave. When they were getting closer to the cave, they didn't see any horses or ladies. Now, they were getting worried about the girls. They noticed their horses were not outside the cave. Maybe, they took a ride and got lost.

The three men dismounted and walked toward the mouth of the cave. When walking inside the cave, they didn't see any evidence anywhere. All they saw was a few feathers to the left of the cave floor. They didn't know why feathers would be in the cave. It was beginning to worry the men who were looking for their guests.

Buzz started to walk out, but Buxton stopped him. "Why did you stop me, Buxton?" Buzz couldn't imagine why he stopped him.

"Why did you stop me?" Buzz was puzzled and didn't know what to say or do. Buzz didn't know why Buxton would tell him to stop. They needed to be looking for the five ladies.

"Come over here. Do you see what I see?" Buck saw what Buxton was talking about.

"I see horse poop," Buzz laughed out loud.

"Let's think this through." Buzz turned on his flashlight. "I'm going to see if there is an opening at the back of the cave."

"Good idea. We'll go with you," Buxton wasn't going to let his brother go alone, because this was beginning to get confusing.

"Surely, they will be back before dark," Buzz thought, for sure, they would be back. This was all confusing to him. They had never had this happen before, but they have time to search before it gets dark.

"It's getting darker. What should we do? We know they didn't leave with the horses at the back of the cave," Buck was agitated as much as the others. "We didn't see a door at the back of the cave." Now, they were truly confused.

Buzz told them to follow him. "We are going to ride around in a large circle," but they didn't even see any horse tracks.

Buck said with reasoning. "We didn't see any tracks. I don't believe this."

"Well, the horses sure didn't fly away," Buck analyzed.

Buzz was friends with the Sheriff, so he called, and the Sheriff brought deputies to help look.

The Sheriff came out of the cave and told them they saw evidence of a small campfire and a few footprints. Some of the prints looked like moccasins and a smaller footprint that looked like a Western boot. The Sheriff told Buzz it could have been someone camping inside the cave.

"Looking at the horse tracks, I would say there were around seven horses in the cave," the Sheriff explained. That was confusing Buzz because we only sent five ladies to the cave unless the camping people were still in there.

"Why would horses be in the cave?" Buck asked with concern, who was confused about this whole situation.

"I would think the horses had been spooked by the storm, and they took them inside. They could have come out after the storm and took a wrong turn," The Sheriff thought all of this was sort of weird. "We can't search now in the dark. It would be better to wait for first light in the morning."

Buzz went back to where Jayne was sitting with tears in her pretty blue eyes. "Honey don't worry. The Sheriff is leaving three of his deputies at the cave tonight to see if they come back."

"Try not to worry. They are smart girls. Who knows? They may have gone back to the house." The ones who went to the store were keeping Jayne company, Buzz put his arm around his wife trying to sooth her. Buzz walked up to the wagon. If his wife had a soft heart, and he knew she was hurting.

Buck walked up to the wagon. "If they come back to the cave, the deputies will take them back to your house.

"Thank you, Buck." Jayne knew the girls were smart, plus they had their guns with them. Some people might not be afraid of women having a gun, because men thought they wouldn't be able to shoot as well as a man.

The Sheriff went to the campsite. He told Buzz and Buxton to go home. If the deputies see the girls, they have orders to escort them back to Buzz and Jayne's house.

"Don't worry, Jayne. We have it covered."

"Thanks, Sheriff," Jayne hoped they had it covered.

Chapter Eleven

Grandee was more than concerned about the missing girls, and not just because her sister, Callie, was with them. She loved them all. She knew they could take care of themselves and each other, but what bothered her most was they were in a territory they knew nothing about.

At least, the missing ladies had their gun, and a flashlight. Grandee knew they wouldn't be afraid. Callie was good at knowing what to do in almost any bad situation. Most of all: Tinker was with them and she has been in the army. She knew much more about camping or hiding behind bushes. Her eyes and ears are keen. She also knew Phoenix could be a good help to them. She is smart, tough, and wise above her years.

"First of all, does everybody have their phone with them? Everybody, call Jayne's number." No one had a signal.

"This means they can't find us. I'm sure they will have someone searching for us," said Olivia.

"Jayne told us earlier that she didn't have a good signal. She said sometimes she has a good signal, but more time than not, she doesn't have one," Jas warned the others.

"I don't want for them to be alone." Olive says.

"I think we should go back to the camp. We will fix supper and then try to get some sleep. Sounds like a good idea," Olive stated.

Other than the girls, Buzz, Buck, and Buxton volunteered to go and stay also. One more night in the outside darkness won't hurt them, plus they would be closer to the Sheriff and his deputies.

The Sheriff would be a bit later due to going back to town to pick up some lanterns and their horses to do a night search. After the search, Sheriff Jones would come back to see if they have had any luck on finding the girls. The girls, who went to the cave, found his lanterns and other things they may need for this situation. They knew someone would rescue them eventually.

Some of the girls were crying while some of them were taking everything in stride. It was like they were not going to let things of importance bother them.

CHAPTER TWELVE

Their host and hostess were upset, but they would be better soon. They trusted the Sheriff. He had helped them with the boys who were vandalizing their barn, and the Sheriff always seemed to fix things. That made them feel much better.

That made the girls, who went to the old Country Store, feel much better about this whole situation. That group could take care of themselves, for sure. They are not mean, but they are just lively ladies.

They knew Phoenix could take care of all of them. Jas always comes up with a way to do anything. Tinker scares people when she puts her ball bat against her shoulder. Olivia can take care if anyone is hurt, and can make them better than ever. Last is Callie. She is just stubborn enough to try things that others can't do. Callie and Olivia are somewhat a little alike. They both are not afraid to do things other people would never try.

Sheriff came up to the group with a silly smile. "One of my deputies told me his wife knows someone who can just feel something and knows who it may be and what they were doing." They were having a hard time believing the Sheriff knew a girl who could help.

"Really, you believe that stuff?" Buxton was somewhat leery about that stuff. "Who knows? The girls may just walk in here in the morning, but even if they don't walk in here in the morning, we will not give up. We don't leave anyone behind."

"Everyone, tell us what you think. Between all of us, surely someone will think of something."

Jayne didn't know what to say. She was still upset that they lost some of the girls.

Grandee said her sister was with them, and she would do whatever everyone wanted to do. Surely, they could think of something to help.

"I think they can take of themselves, and they will come back on their own," Alaska gave her opinion. Alaska was right about the girls taking care of themselves.

"I don't know what to think. I'm upset my cousins are missing," Olive still had tears in her eyes. Houston went to Olive and put her arm around her to give her some calmness.

Houston had her opinion, "It couldn't hurt anything and may be worth a try to go with the deputy's wife."

"Do we do this thing in day or night?" Grandee asked.

The deputy, whose wife is the Fortune Teller, called this so-called Fortune Teller and told him they should wait until morning.

"Okay, everyone, meet at eight in the morning to have a good breakfast, and we can leave from there. They all went toward their beds.

CHAPTER THIRTEEN

The confused time-travelers jumped on their horses and rode to the town. Off went five women, two Indian Chiefs, and one small man.

When they finally made it to the small town. A man came out of a tiny building that had the word 'Sheriff' over the door. The man with a star on his lapel said, "Sir, may I get your names? We don't just let anybody in our little town. "We are not mean people. We don't need to worry about us."

Callie looked at the stocky Sheriff with a big hat and told him the little one over there is William H. Bonney.

They could all see that this didn't sit well with the short Sheriff, who wears a tall cowboy hat that is too big for his head.

"No, we don't want Billy the Kid here in our happy town shooting people." Billy looked aggravated because he hadn't even drawn his gun in several days.

The five ladies were shocked to have such a historical figure among them. "Wait a minute, what century are we in?" Callie asked with a smile. She knew she wasn't in Kansas anymore.

The Sheriff had a countenance of disbelief on his face. "We are in the eighteen hundreds."

"We live in 2024 in your future," Jas said with clarification. Everyone around the Sheriff that heard that last comment Jas made were scared and in disbelief.

Women on the sidewalk strolled around in their long gingham dresses with bonnets on their heads. People were looking at the girls in their jeans and laughing at them. The girls couldn't blame the people who were laughing at them.

It didn't bother the ladies. "We would think the same thing and be laughing too if we were the ones people were laughing at.

The Sheriff was looking like he didn't know whether to shoot someone or put them all in jail. He had never been this confused before. The Sheriff looked at the Indians. "Where did you pick up the two Indians?"

"Well, the Cherokee with the big mouth is 'He Who Wanders'," Billy explained. "The Choctaw is his friend, and his name is 'Big Moon',"

The Indians told them they traveled back and forth. The girls thought they needed to talk to the Indians. They could ask them how to get back to Jayne and Buzz's house.

"I think we are all tired. Why don't we find somewhere to sleep," Tinker said with a big yawn. The Sheriff overheard the ladies talking about a place to sleep. "Ladies, if I may, we have a hotel, but it is filled up right now."

"Jake has plenty of room in the stable," The Sheriff smiled at the girls. They didn't seem to like the idea, but they were tired enough to sleep anywhere.

"Oh yeah, I forgot, that would be ten bits for the night," The Sheriff was loving this.

"If the ladies don't have the money, you will go to the Saloon and work until you get the money. You are all pretty enough to get good tips."

"Okay, girls, let's go to work," said Olivia as she threw out a sweet smile. She wasn't too keen on working in a Saloon, but she sure was tired enough to do whatever they needed to do. The bartender told the ladies to just smile, and they will give you a good tip.

CHAPTER FOURTEEN

The five tired ladies and one Bill the Kid sat wondering what to do next. They looked around in the town. The two Indian Chiefs sat side by side as they watched Billy draw his gun. They sure didn't want to be shot by Billy the Kid. He didn't pull the trigger, but he just was only practicing how quick he could draw his gun. The girls were amazed at how Billy could draw his gun.

Billy sat staring at the girls. His Mama would never have been caught without a dress on her body, but he figured that is what ladies do now. He still couldn't get an idea of why a woman would wear a pair of pants. Although, the pants would be good for riding a horse. That's why all these ladies have on their britches.

The girls were the first ones to notice the Indians were beginning to get antsy. The girls thought this couldn't be good. That is when the Indian Chiefs began to argue with each other.

The Cherokee said, "You stupid. You say we are in the 1700's."

The Choctaw grunted and said, "No you stupid. Me smart." The Cherokee tried to explain.

The Cherokee says, "I knock you on butt."

The girls and even Billy were all laughing at the banter the Indians were doing back and forth. They all thought it was sort of funny to listen to them. The girls sure didn't want to make Billy mad at them, so they decided not to tease him anymore.

The Indians looked at the five ladies and couldn't believe what they were seeing.

Fat Indian say girls dress funny. The girls were thinking they didn't need someone who wore feathers on their head to give them ideas on their way of dressing. They all started laughing.

"Where we sleep tonight, Fatso," Cherokee Chief says with a smile on his rugged face.

Choctaw had a snarl on his face, "You sleep with pigs."

The banter between the two Indians were keeping them all entertained all day and night.

The girls decided they should have a better name for the Indian Chiefs.

"I have an idea," Phoenix said with a silly giggle.

"What do you think, ladies?" Jas says with another giggle.

"I think we should call them 'John' and the other one should be 'Wayne'. Olivia was on the ball. She didn't know if the others would go with that or not, but she really did like John Wayne.

Callie looked at the other ladies and told them they needed to stick with a part of their tribes. "I suggest we call them 'Choc' and 'Kee'.

"Okay with me," Tinker said. She was just glad to be there with her friends. Everybody thought it was good names for their friends, the Indian Chiefs.

They all noticed that both Chiefs were laying on the floor of the cave fast asleep. They figured the Chiefs didn't care what their names were.

Chapter Fifteen

Billy told everyone he will see if he could get the stable to sleep in tonight. He figured these girls had never slept in a stable before in their lives. Billy kept staring at the girls. He kept smiling at them. He wondered why they even came in that cave. He couldn't believe how they were dressed. He also saw each of the ladies had a pistol. He sure wasn't going to be mean to those ladies.

"I have a question," Jas asked. Jas couldn't believe she was really talking to Billy the Kid from the 1800's.

"How do we get back to Oklahoma and to the house where they were visiting?

The Cherokee Indian Chief answered with one word, 'Lightening'?

"Do you mean we can't get back until there is another storm?" Tinker was somewhat confused, but she was hoping it would be soon no matter what time it is, or how we get there.

"You are right," Choctaw Chief smiled as he shook his head dropping feathers out of his head dress all over the floor of the stable.

They heard the door to the stable opening. The Sheriff walked in with his gun out of its holster. "I'm here to take Billy. Someone shot the bartender last night. Billy, did you shoot him?"

"I did not," Billy said with a crooked smile.

Olivia looked at the Sheriff. "Billy has been in the stable with us all night. It couldn't have been Billy. We heard him snoring all night long.

All the ladies along with two Indian Chiefs stood up for Billy. "Girl was right. You wrong."

The Indian Chiefs thought the Sheriff a little crazy. The girls walked over to Billy and stood in front of him. They knew he had been asleep all night.

"Okay, if that's what you want, come with me," The stocky Sheriff said. "I'm putting all of you in the jail."

"You are making a big mistake. Billy was with us all night," Phoenix said.

"We do not kill anyone," The Chiefs said, even Billy didn't. He was sleeping much too loudly.

"The ladies are right. We stayed awake all night. We no sleep. Billy sleep loud."

"I don't believe any of you. Come, or I will shoot you," The irritated Sheriff said in a loud voice. The Sheriff was somewhat confused as to what to do with all these people. The Sheriff was showing signs of irritation. No one wanted to go to the jail, but they didn't think they had a choice. Maybe, they wouldn't have to stay too long. They wanted to go back to the ranch they came from.

CHAPTER SIXTEEN

The Fortune Teller came the next morning to Buzz's house. The girls were hopeful this lady can do what she says she can do. They were ready to find out about where the cave people may be. They knew they couldn't find them with their phones because they don't have a signal, especially in a cave. They would wait until someone came to rescue them.

The lady, who came to help, said she would help them out. The deputies, girls, Jayne, Buzz, and Buxton all went because this was something they had never done before. Some of them were having trouble believing this lady could really help them. The others thought it just might work. They are the positive people. It won't hurt to try her.

The searchers were filled with carefree hearts along with hope. They didn't have any clue where they could be. The Country Store girls didn't like not knowing where the girls could be, or if they were okay.

They had a good idea that the cave girls would be okay. Between them, they knew they could survive.

The lady, whose name was Moonbeam, told the others she was ready to begin. They had several lanterns, so they could see everywhere in the cave. That was a plus. It would have to be horrible if there was no light.

Moonbeam, who was dressed like a gypsy, was ready to begin. She walked around before touching anything.

Moonbeam saw the remains of a small campfire. She walked to where the campfire was located. She touched some logs that was still in the campfire.

The campfire was cold and not been used in quite a while. She said something next that the search party couldn't understand. Someone from the past had been here.

They had already noticed that seven horses had been in the cave. She told the others the horses went out of the back of the cave, which was more confusing to the searchers.

Next, she went to a ledge in the wall of the cave. There are moccasin prints. Looks like two sets of moccasin prints. I see many feathers like what an Indian Chief would wear.

There was a storm yesterday. After the horses came in, I see a white cloud. Five women, one small man, and two Indian Chiefs walked away inside the white cloud.

"What are you talking about?" Buzz asked. They all were all becoming confused.

"I have an idea that they have had a strange thing happen to them," said the lady named Moonbeam.

"What are you talking about?" Buzz asked. All that were confused couldn't wait to hear what she had to say."

"This is a magic cave. Several people are missing after they went in the cave. What I saw about the white cloud makes me think they have traveled back in time," Moonbeam looked at the ones sitting there to see if they think she is crazy.

The friends of all the ones who are missing say when they were lost, it was a bad storm outside. The day the girls were at the cave there was a bad storm."

"This sounds a little far-fetched, but we need to try anything we can," Buzz said, and the others agreed.

"Thank you, Miss Moonbeam. We have a lot to think about. We will go back to the house and discuss these things you showed us. There much be a connection somewhere between all you have told us.

CHAPTER SEVENTEEN

The sleepy ladies ambled to the Happy Slappy Saloon. Everyone in the room was looking at the five ladies with the strange clothes. The bartender saw the ladies come in the Happy Slappy. He knew why they were there. He moseyed to the back room where the clothes were kept.

The bartender came back with five dresses. The girls began to chuckle at all the sparkly dresses. He threw Tinker a blue dance hall dress. Tinker didn't know what to do when she put her dress on because she was so tall, it showed a good portion of her long legs. Then she figured no one would look at her legs anyway.

Jas was given a bright red dress along with a headband with red feathers on top. Jas started laughing at her dress and feathers. She would just go along with it for now. She sure didn't want anyone to see her in this weird dress. She really didn't wear dresses too much anyway.

Olivia had a short yellow dress with birds on it. She laughed when she saw all the birds. It had to be the most hideous dress in the whole wide world. She couldn't wait to get this unappealing thing over and done with. She came up with an idea. She would wear her pants under the dress.

The bartender threw Phoenix a black dress with white diamonds on it. Tinker knew that was rhinestones on the dress. She thought no one in their right mind would put that many diamonds on this frumpy dress.

Callie thought she was going to get out of dressing like a lady of the night until the bartender brought her a burgundy dress with fur around the neckline. She thought it was a horrible dress, and she didn't want anything about it near her.

While they were getting into their work clothes, they could hear the music that was coming from the old-timey piano. The girls would never hear the song 'Buffalo Gal, Won't You Come Out Tonight' in the same way ever again. This whole thing was degrading.

Five men walked over to dance with the girls. The girls' noticed Tinker was dancing with a man who was her height. They also noticed that Tinker still had her ball bat on her shoulder. She looked somewhat out of place, but it didn't seem to upset anyone. Some of the men was wondering why a woman would have a stick on her shoulder while dancing, but they didn't say anything about it.

When the music stopped, the ladies were relieved. Now, maybe they are finished and can go back to the stable. They couldn't wait to get out of their grotesque outfits.

When the man saw Tinker and Phoenix with their weapons, he went back and sat down. He figured he didn't want any of that. This was the worst dancing girls he had ever seen.

The bartender told the ladies to be his waitresses. They were told to take the beer to the tables. Callie had a man hit her on the behind, and she pushed his chair over on the floor with him in it. He left the Bar soon after his little accident with a girl.

He jumped up and was going to attack Callie, but he stopped when he saw three pistols, and one big stick up in the air. The man didn't know what to think about these ladies. He had never seen anything like it before. What was this world coming to if ladies of the evening started beating up on men?

The tips they made was the only thing good about their little adventure. The girls took a break to count their money and changed back in their strange clothes with them giggling at what they had done that night. The Indians and Billy sure would have liked to see what happened with the girls that night.

Jas told the ladies to stop what they were doing. "We need to think about something. We are going to jail for killing the bartender and the bartender is pouring drinks in the bar tonight." They were too busy, to think about that.

Chapter Eighteen

Billy told the others he was going to see if he could get them in the stable for the night. Billy was staring at the funny-dressed girls. He couldn't take his eyes off them. He couldn't believe how they were dressed. He knew they had pistols and a ball bat, so he wouldn't bother them.

Billy wanted to know something, "I hear you ladies had a little tussle last night. We were wondering if you ladies were hurt. If you are, let us know and we will take care of it."

"It wasn't anything we couldn't handle," Phoenix said with a silly smile. the girl cousins are proud of how they can take care of themselves.

Jas looked at everyone in the room, "Billy, I thought you would be a little taller."

"What you see is what you get, Darlin'. No, I'm not too tall, but I don't have trouble with anyone," Billy explained. "I can take care of myself also."

Billy didn't know how he ever got in the cave. He was just trying to get out of the storm. The lightning was horrific. The Indians were already there chanting in some sort of language. He didn't know why they were there, but he would find out later.

"Billy, do you know you are in history," Jas said hoping Billy would understand. He made a face like he really didn't know what Jas was talking about.

"So, tell me about some things they say about me." He really didn't know if he wanted to know about himself or not.

"We know you were born in 1859 and you have Irish roots, but your family went west at some point. Jas was liking talking to Billy. She always liked to know about things in history.

"You were alleged to have killed twenty-one men. You are known to be quick as a flash with a gun." Billy smiled at that one. He knew he was fast, but he wasn't too sure about killing that many men. He never shot anyone who didn't need it, or he was defending himself.

"I have a question for you. Do you know when I died and how did I die?" Billy really didn't think he would want to know this, or not. He would have to put more thought into this.

Jas looked Billy in the eyes." Do you really want to know?"

"Well, maybe not." Billy just hung his head and wouldn't look at the girls.

"Thank you, Jas, for talking to me." Jas was glad he didn't want to know about his death. She knew she couldn't change history.

Chapter Nineteen

The girls in their cell sat giggling about all that has happened so far on this trip. They never thought they would be in the pokey while on vacation. At least, they feed them good in here, but it's not as good as what Jayne has been cooking. Hopefully, they will be back at Buzz and Jayne's soon. It's kind of weird that we can't get back without a storm. Perhaps, the cave was magic.

The Deputy and the Sheriff hobbled into the jail with three men. The Deputy went over to an empty cell and told the three men to get in the cell. One of the men made a break for the front door. The Deputy started running and jumped on top of the running man tackling him to the floor. The man arose from the floor. After using a strong expletive, he went inside with his two friends.

One of the man's friends noticed Olivia in the next cell and winked at her. Olivia looked like she was going to get up and beat him with Tinker's big stick. At least, that is what the men around there thought it was.

"What you in here for, little darlin'?" The running man asked.

"Well, I guess we are in here for nothing," Olivia didn't exactly know why they were there. This was getting more confusing the longer they stayed in this small jail cell.

We are just visiting this little town and I guess they didn't like us and threw us in this stinky jail.

The Sheriff, who had gone to the Diner, to tell the cooks they needed to bring food for eleven people.

"WOW! Sheriff, you have been busy. I'll tell them, and they will get on that pretty soon."

The Sheriff saw old Lady Pearl and he walked over to her and told her she had to come to the jail. "We have been searching for you." The Sheriff thought he had his chance to get Miss Pearl, and he didn't want that chance to go away.

The old woman sure didn't want to go to jail, so she started running as fast as a ninety-year-old woman could run. The Sheriff wasn't an experienced runner, but he was a touch faster than Pearl.

When the Sheriff opened the door, Miss Pearl took off down the hall. The Sheriff caught her and shoved her in the cell with her screaming to the top of her lungs.

Everyone in their cells were laughing. The Deputy looked around the cells and noticed they didn't have any more empty cells. That was just his luck to finally catching Pearl, and now he had no cell for her.

Jas looked at the Deputy right before she said, "Miss Pearl can stay with us in our cell. We would love to have her."

Deputy Do put Miss Pearl in the girl's cell. Phoenix looked at Pearl and asked her why they put her in jail. Pearl gave the girls a huge silly grin.

"Well, it was just a little thing. It had to be done, and I am the one to do it." Miss Pearl had a smile on her wrinkled face. The girls were still amazed that a woman that old could outrun a man.

"Miss Pearl, just what was so important that you had to do something so bad, it put you in jail?" Callie was interested. She liked older people, and she didn't like to see older people in jail. She really didn't want to see anyone in jail, but here they were in a jail cell.

"My husband used to beat me because he didn't like that I talked to the chickens when I was going to gather the eggs. I mean something had to be done, so I had to do my duty. I thought it was nice of me to bury him under the old oak tree in the backyard. It's a right pretty tree."

CHAPTER TWENTY

The girls, who were with Jayne, were still a little turned upside down. They didn't have a clue where they could be. They were trying as hard as they could to stay positive. They knew the girls could take care of themselves, or they may be somewhere having a grand ole time. If the girls ever see anything that looks fun, they jump in and have fun.

Jayne and the Country Store girls would find them sooner or later. They just prayed it would be sooner. Jayne and the store girls all started praying they would find their cousins.

Buzz sent Buck to retrieve the girls, so they can go in the big house to discuss a few things. They walked to the house not knowing what Buzz and Jayne were going to say. They were praying the missing girls were sitting in their living room, but that wasn't going to be.

Buzz stood up. Everyone heard what Moonbeam said. "We have a lot to talk about. We heard a lot, and it was a lot to take in. Someone had made a campfire in that cave. It was a cold fire so he must have been there a while. They hoped for a nice person to be in the cave. They sure didn't want them kidnapped or harmed in any way. If they are harmed then the girls would take over."

The girls along with Jayne mounted their horses to see if they could find any clues that the girls were there. They rode to the cave. They went inside the cave, so they could go search the back of the cave. The ladies searched and searched for footprints. Now, they rode around to the back of the cave. There were absolutely no prints anywhere and no opening that they could find. If there was another door in the back of the cave, it must be covered very well.

They all were thinking this was a confusing state of affairs. They had been in situations such as these, but they still pray for the best.

Perhaps, there are bushes that cover the opening. If there were bushes, they are having a hard time finding them.

"We need to get off our horse and look through the bushes. You would think we would find some litter or something." Jayne felt sorry for the girls, but she would do whatever she needed, so they could be happier. They felt better when they were searching something.

"I don't believe all this," Houston was another one who likes their adventures. "It looks like if they came out of the back, wouldn't we see horse tracks?"

"Maybe, unless they wiped them away with something," Alaska said with authority. The others thought they probably wouldn't try to spend the time searching for something that wasn't there.

"Why would they leave the cave?" Jayne asked.

"They may have waited out the storm, and then took a walk."

Chapter Twenty-One

"How about we try to make an escape plan. We are smart and can think of something," Olivia thought that was a grand idea. She sure didn't like the idea of the ladies leaving the cave on their horses without making tracks.

"I saw on TV during a Western one time where they put a rope on the bars of the window and pulled the bars with a wagon. We can crawl out the window," Tinker said with a silly smile. She really didn't think they could do that, but they are ready to try anything.

"I don't think that would work too well because jumping out a window wouldn't work. There are too many of us, and we would be caught. I agree with Callie," Olivia said.

Jas has an idea. "One of us can say they need to go to the bathroom. When she walks back, she quietly gets the keys off the nail and unlocks the cell doors. We need to do it when the Deputy Do, and the Sheriff are gone."

Jas was the one who renamed him to Deputy Do.

"That might work," Phoenix said with a giggle. She was more than ready to break out of this horrible cell.

Phoenix looked at the others with a smile. "I feel like I'm in Mayberry. The keys are on the wall by the cells on a nail on the dirty walls. All they needed would be a Barney Fife.

When Phoenix finished, she turned around and Billy the Kid was standing outside the cell. "How did you get out?"

"Don't you know? I am good at getting out of jails." Billy gave a silly laugh. That much be in history."

"I have a question," Billy says. They couldn't imagine what he wanted to know now.

Tinker said something about watching a TV.

"What's a TV?" Billy didn't have a clue what a TV could be. He was getting confused now.

"It's sort of a box that has a picture on it. You can see people walking around and can hear them talk," Tinker hoped she said it so he could understand.

Chapter Twenty-Two

After Billy let everybody out of their cell, the Sheriff and Deputy Do came back to the office. They looked around and wondered how they got out. The Sheriff always heard about Billy the Kid being good at getting out of jails, but he never thought he would be in his jail. He was wishing Billy would just jump on his horse and go somewhere else.

The Sheriff and Deputy Do did a search for the rest of the day to find their prisoners. They noticed one was missing. Miss Pearl could not be found. The Sheriff was a touch scared to go to find Miss Pearl because if she gets mad at him, she may shoot him and plant him under the big oak tree by her dearly departed husband.

The prisoners knew this was a small town and not many places to hide. They finally found a farmhouse with a bright blue door. Someone from the house had put two apple pies on the window to cool off. They thought this must be a good place to stay for a while because they were beginning to have hunger pains just smelling the apple pies.

The house had a bright blue door. It also had a big barn they may stay in for a while. They stayed in the barn for two nights. It was a good place because there were lots of stalls for their horses. They stayed two nights without the people in the house even knowing they were there.

They decided to go back toward town. It is where they need to be due to knowing which way to go for the cave. They put on disguises with the ladies wearing long gingham dresses and bonnets. The girls didn't want to steal the dresses off the clothesline, but they would leave them before going back to the cave.

They found what looked like an abandoned building. It was dark in the building, but they went in anyway. They all looked around and saw several caskets. One of the girls looked at the words over the door. '*Undertaker.*' "Wow, y'all know that we are in here with dead people in the caskets, don't you.

Billy and the Indian Chiefs slept by a casket with a man whose wife stuck a pitchfork in her husband. They were hoping the wife wouldn't come back to get his body. She didn't seem to be the kind of woman they wanted to meet.

Another casket had a man that had been shot, but it turned out, the man wasn't dead at all. They took him out of the casket. Surely, we can find a better place than this. They put him in a dirty chair so they could talk to him.

They all agreed to find a better place. Maybe, we could sneak back in the stable and leave for the cave the next morning before daylight. That was what they wanted to do, and they would make it happen.

The Sheriff may see us leave, but then again, he probably wants us to leave. We have made a few problems for the Sheriff and Deputy Do.

Chapter Twenty-Three

The girls, Jayne, Buzz, Buxton, and Buck was thinking of something to make the girls forget the problem. They didn't want to see them sad, but they understood why. All these ladies, who were missing, are all cousins. The irritated girls were trying their best to not be a gracious grumpy.

The girl cousins began talking about the adventures they have had during their holidays. "Please don't leave anything out," Jayne wanted to hear it all. She had heard some of their adventures and they were great. She could sit and listen to them all day and night. She didn't know how they got in those situations, but she knew the cousins would do the rescue.

"We were on an adventure something like this is now. We were in Boston and in a museum. There was construction, and there was a large hole in the floor. We all fell into the hole. When we woke up, we were in a pub in 1773 Boston right before the revolutionary war started. We met Samuel Adams, and other founding fathers. Houston got a boyfriend. When I say boyfriend, I mean he wasn't but around twenty or less. We try our best not to tease her, but sometimes we forget. She is always laughing about it, and she doesn't become mad when all her cousins tease her."

"We have had so many adventures, but we managed to come out the winner. We thought since everyone is getting a little older that they need to do their adventures now," Alaska said with a large smile.

"Thank you for making us laugh. It made us feel much better," Alaska said with a giggle. Not many women have had adventures such as ours. We still have lots of fun on our vacations, even though we never know what we might find.

"Jayne, maybe you could go with us on one of our vacations. They have been adventurous, to say the least." Jayne's eyes lit up when Olive said she could go with them. Buzz didn't know what to say, but he would let Jayne do what she wanted. He knew she worked here at the ranch and needed a break every now and then.

"We really should feel better. We shouldn't worry about the other girls because all five of them can do a lot of stuff to protect themselves." Olive worries sometimes, but she gets over it and laughs like the others.

"You need to feel better. We shouldn't worry about the other girls because all five of them can do a lot of damage in a short amount of time. They are all smart and can figure out what to do in a crisis.

"You will love this. We don't need something fancy to take someone down. Just ask Phoenix. She used an iron skillet on a man." They all laughed at that. Buzz said he sure would like to have seen that little episode.

"Buzz, would you be willing to cook your own food and do the dishes if I went on a trip with these wonderful ladies?"

"I can take care of myself. I sure would miss you though, but you deserve a break too," Buzz assured he would be okay.

"You could go only if you called me every night to see how you were. With these ladies, you never know what might happen, but I would know they would take care of the situation."

"You got that right, Buzz," Houston said with a silly grin. "We don't play around when there is a cousin, friend, or even a family member to rescue.

Chapter Twenty-Four

The Sheriff and Deputy Do found their prisoners and took them back to their cells. "Go in and have a seat. I have some food ordered for you. I figured we would find you. There are just so many places to hide, and they are not good ones either." The Sheriff smiled at the run-away prisoners.

After you finish your food, I am going to pull my chair closer to you. I think it is time to tell us about yourselves and how you got here. I know you were riding horses, and that's about all I know.

"Before you start, I believe we are missing someone. Where is our friend Billy the Kid?" The Sheriff has a good memory under the large cowboy hat he wears.

"Billy said he wouldn't be going back with us. I think he said something about going West," Jas says. "We will pray for his time traveling."

"Okay, what about you?" The two Indians started talking, and he thought they would never shut up. He couldn't make any sense of their conversations, but they acted like they knew what they were saying. They didn't want to hurt their feelings.

"I Indian Chief. Cherokee. I go home."

"I'm Choctaw. Me smart. He crazy."

"Okay, which of you ladies want to talk? Jas started, "We were staying with friends in Oklahoma. We were riding and went in a cave. Billy had already been there along with the two Indian Chiefs. I think they are harmless. They fuss with each other, at times, but they are truly friends who like to tease each other."

"We went in the cave. It started raining, and then the loud noise of thunder was heard. Our horses were getting spooked by the thunder, so we took them in the cave. Before we knew what was happening, a strike of bright lightning struck instantly, and something like a thick white cloud surrounded us. When it was over, we were out of the cave and looking at your little town."

"This story is a little unbelievable, but stranger things have happened," The Sheriff was amazed. Not much made him amazed, but this one was a wonder.

"The cave we were in is called a magic cave. We don't believe it, but here we are."

"All we want is to go back to our friends, family, and the rest of our cousins," Callie said. She, along with the rest, couldn't wait. She knew the others at the ranch would be worried.

"I wish you a safe journey. You are free to go. I have heard of that cave. I didn't know it had magical powers. Good Luck!" The Sheriff walked back to check on things in the jail while shaking his head.

Chapter Twenty-Five

The Sheriff and Deputy Do ambled slowly behind the girls out the old wooden door that had seen better days. They began talking about what they had just heard from the girls, and two Indian Chiefs. The girls didn't blame the Sheriff for not believing about the cave and its magic powers. The story was a little out there, but it made for a good story.

At least, the food is decent in here, but they would rather be back at Buzz and Jayne's house. They knew their cousins would be worried about them. They sure didn't want to make them worry about them. They have enough on them.

The jail wasn't too clean, but Lord only knows, how old it is. The planks on the wall were beginning to show some wear and tear. When they looked around everywhere they noticed the stores were in the same shape as the jailhouse. They can truly say they were in an Old Western town. They knew no one would believe them, and they hardly could believe it himself.

The Sheriff and Deputy Do came back in the jailhouse with good news. They had made a little stop at the Happy Slappy Saloon. The girls were praying they needed any more dancing girls, because we didn't do so well the last time we danced.

Girls and Chiefs, after going in the Saloon found out the bartender wasn't even dead. They couldn't imagine how that happened. Someone must have given wrong information. They hadn't even heard a gunshot since they came to this town. We don't even know the name of this town.

One of the men sitting playing poker heard what they were talking about and hollered, "This town's name is Hogwaller."

"So, I guess Billy the Kid didn't kill the bartender, or anyone else in this town," The Sheriff explained."

"Sheriff, as soon as we finish our food, can we go to the stable and fetch our horses?" Phoenix asked. She was still smiling to know the town's name was Hogwaller. The girls were laughing because they had never heard Phoenix say she was going to fetch something. Another thing that amazed them, was why anyone would name a town Hogwaller.

"I can help with the town name. Years ago, hogs were everywhere running around on the streets making a mess when it rained. The hogs would waller down in the mud and be just as happy as can be. Of course, this is a story my grandpappy told me when I was a boy.

Little ladies, I'm sorry we made a mistake about the bartender," The Sheriff had a look on his face making him know he did something wrong.

"It's okay, Mr. Sheriff, you are a busy man and have things to do. Don't worry about it," Jas explained with a giggle.

"How about I go with you to the cave? I want to make sure you are alright," Sheriff explained. The girls thought that was so nice of him wanting to make sure they got to the right place.

They made it to the cave without any trouble. They told the Sheriff and Deputy Do goodbye. The Sheriff said, "Be careful. It looks like it may be a storm coming in." The girls and Indians couldn't wait to return to the real cave they came from. They were beginning to be excited about seeing everyone at the ranch.

The Sheriff and Deputy Do left the cave. They all looked around and noticed someone was missing. Where could Tinker have gone?

Chapter Twenty-Six

"Did anyone see if Tinker got on the wrong trail? I didn't see her get on another trail." Billy said.

"How could someone not be able to see her as tall as Tinker is? She rides well on her horse." They hoped her horse didn't buck her off. She may be out there all alone and hurt. They sure didn't want to even think for a minute that Tinker may be hurt.

"You're right. We need to go search for her," Callie says with concern. Callie and the girls would never leave anyone, especially in the situation they are in now. They knew if it was any one of us out here maybe lost and hurt, Tinker would be the first one on her horse to find them. Tinker is a good friend, and the girls were sad about her situation.

Jas looked up at the clouds which looked like a storm may be coming just like the Sheriff said.

Everyone looked up to see what Jas was looking at. The raindrops were starting to come down to the dry earth. This could be their chance to get back to the cave and on to Buzz and Jayne's ranch.

"This was our chance to leave and go back to Buzz and Jayne's house," Alaska said with a sad face. "This may be our only chance to go back.

Olivia put her hand on Callie's arm, "This is not the end of the world. If we need to wait for another storm, we will wait. One thing we won't do, is we won't go anywhere without all our group. Let's do some searching, ladies."

The rain was pouring down on the cold ladies. They didn't have raincoats or any way to be warmer. Perhaps, they could make a fire when they get in the cave.

Phoenix looked at everyone sitting in the saddle ready to do whatever they could do to find Tinker. "We need to think about something. This heavy rain may make the footprints or horse tracks go away."

"You're right, Phoenix. Maybe, we could find somewhere to find shelter and wait out the storm," Callie thought it was a good idea.

The girls began their search for some sort of shelter. The rain was still pouring down like someone was pouring it out of a large bucket.

Olivia told the gang to look to the right. They all saw it at the same time. It seemed to be an abandoned cabin by a few trees. "It's not much, but it might keep the rain off us," Callie glanced at the cabin that appeared it could be on the ground at any minute.

"Listen, ladies. It is worth it to give it a try. It may be better than it looks." Jas was somewhat leery of the antique cabin, but she wanted to give it the others some hope.

"I'm in," Callie says. "Come on, it can't be all bad. It will have a fireplace, and we need to get warmed up. Who knows? It may be a good adventure.

The rest of the ladies followed Callie. It did give them a touch of hope. Jas can always give them interesting ways to feel better.

CHAPTER TWENTY-SEVEN

William H. Bonney A.K.A. Billy the Kid began thinking about the ladies who dressed funny. He wondered if the two old Indians were taking care of these ladies. He really thought the Indians would not do that. Perhaps, he should go back and take care of them, and get to know them better. He felt bad about leaving the girls. He wanted to see if they were alright.

They didn't hurt anyone. Maybe, he should apologize for leaving them in the jail. He knew he could have gotten them out, but every time he broke out of a jail, the posse always was on his tail, whether he did something wrong or not. He already had a bad reputation.

He heard of the Lincoln County War, and he went to help. He was one of Tunstall cowboys, who called themselves Regulators.

Jas looked out what she thought was sort of a window. "Girls, come look out. That's Billy. He may have seen the cabin and got the same idea we did. Someone needs to open the door for Billy.

Phoenix walked over the door, opened it, and let Billy inside the cabin. The girls found several dry logs to make a fire, so it was comfortable inside.

"Billy, we wondered where you went when you got out of jail," Olivia asked with a sneaky smile. Her mom and her sisters and brothers all had sneaky smiles, but they loved them all.

"I went to be a Regulator in the Lincoln County War," Billy said with a smile.

"WOW! That sounds scary," Jas was throwing out a huge sneaky smile. She was loving this. No one would believe her if she told it.

Billy told the others that he wasn't going back in the cave. He will stay here in this time where he belongs. "I know you are wanting back home, but don't worry. There are usually lots of storms this time of the year."

"Thanks, Billy, that gives us some hope," Olivia says. They had to get their hope where they could get it. They girls thought things were beginning to look up. Having Billy with them made them more confident they would see the cave soon.

Billy began talking about another reason he came back. "Ladies, I felt bad about leaving you at the jail. I wanted to come back and make sure you were okay. I will stay to make sure you get home. I figured the big Indian Chiefs wouldn't help any. They do argue a lot, and that takes up most of their time."

Billy glanced at the ladies and noticed how upset all of them were, "You may be in luck because it has stopped raining. I have one more thing that may have happened. There is a Creek Camp close by. One of the Creek Indians may have taken her. Don't worry. They are somewhat friendly. She may have been thrown from her horse. It is better to be taken by the Creeks than outlaws. I will help you search. I don't like the idea of one woman being riding alone in that area. There are snakes, outlaws, and Indians. The Creek Indians would be the best. It is also if a snake spooked a horse, it may have bucked her off."

"When can we start?" Olivia asked Billy.

"I think we should get a good night's sleep. We will be more rested in the morning. I know the country and can help you find Tinker."

"Thanks, Billy," Jas smiled. She thought things were looking well for them all. Jas couldn't believe Billy had such a bad reputation because he had been so nice to them, but to be honest, that was a different time and place.

"Girls, I would like to say that it is a pleasure to meet all of you, and Tinker when we find her, and we will. I know you ladies may dress funny, but all of you have a good heart, and I like that you do."

"Don't worry about me, I don't rob trains or banks for a living. Oh maybe, I might steal a horse or two, but nothing too bad," Billy liked these ladies and wanted them to like him. Most women stay away from him.

Chapter Twenty-Eight

Tinker awoke on the wet ground. It took her a moment to remember what happened to her. It was getting clearer now that she was trying her best to find out what happened. It was almost there. She didn't like not knowing what happened, or where the other girls were. She knew she would remember eventually.

She remembered a snake spooking her horse making the horse run faster. That was when she fell into a deep hole. She was holding on tightly. When the horse bucked, Tinker was hoping Grandee wasn't around when the snake came around. She knew Grandee was horrified at the thoughts of a snake, much less, seeing one too close.

At the same time, Tinker was in the deep hole, the girls were mounting their horses. The ladies knew they wouldn't leave Tinker. "She may not be far from us." She may even turn around and find them. It was a stretch, but they were thinking it all with a positive attitude.

Tinker woke from another nap, she didn't know where she was, or how she got there. She didn't realize it, but her eyes closed for another nap. All she really knew was when someone would come rescue her. She knew the girls would be searching. She was hoping, at least, one of the ladies would think to bring a rope since they didn't know what kind of situation she may be having.

While searching for Tinker, Billy picked up something he had never seen before. Phoenix picked it up and explained it was used in a baseball game during our time. "Tinker is never without it. It's her weapon instead of a gun. She didn't really want to use a gun. She preferred her trusty old ball-bat to be her only weapon instead of a gun."

Billy saw a few tracks the rain didn't get rid of. He didn't like where they were leading and told the ladies the tracks were leading toward the Creek Nation. That didn't make the ladies happy. The two old Indian Chiefs they met were harmless. They were sure the Creek Indians would be harmless too, or Billy wouldn't have come there.

Jas picked up Tinker's ball bat and put it on her horse where the rifle should be. They were hoping they would find a healthy lady. They didn't want to even think that she might be hurt badly.

Chapter Twenty-Nine

The ladies and Billy the Kid were talking and decided they would go to the Creek Indians to see if they have seen Tinker, or if they had her. They were praying for the best outcome. The girls sure didn't want their friend, Tinker, to be harmed in any way while in the Indian camp.

The time-traveling ladies were taking great pains to be quiet as they approached the camp of the Creek Indians. Billy wasn't too nervous about going to find Tinker. He was being cavalier about it all.

The girls were very nervous about what they may see when they find Tinker. They wanted to see how Tinker was doing. If the Indians wanted us out of here, we wouldn't have a sporting chance of outrunning them. The Indians were benevolent right now. If they wanted to give chase, they would have done it by now. Billy knew more about the Creek Indians than the girls knew.

"Don't worry, ladies. I know the Indians, and they are not too violent," Billy was trying to make the girls feel better. The girls didn't expect to see painted faces. They thought painted faces were just for war.

Someone came out of the house, which was pole frames covered in mud or grass or bark roofs. The garb he was wearing was somewhat colorful complete with red stripes painted on his rugged face. He looked somewhat scary, but the Brave assured them he wasn't a bad Indian.

The Indian walked to the ladies and Billy. "Hello, Mr. Billy. What you want?" The Chief was the colorful one. The ones, who were searching for Tinker, couldn't believe that Billy was so welcomed in the Creek Nation. Apparently, Billy and the Chief were friends. This made the ladies smile to know they finally had found their friend, Tinker.

Billy looked the Chief in the eyes. "We wanted to know if there was a tall woman here that was hurt," Chief pointed to the huge house in the middle of the others. This made the ladies smile to know they finally had found their friend, Tinker.

"Yes, she was hurt. We did not do it. She fell off horse and hurt her head. I put her horse tied to a tree. You will find her horse next to the Chief's house when she is able to ride. We won't stop you when you go. I will tell Braves not to bother any of you.

When the ladies went inside the house, if you could call it that, where the Chief pointed. They noticed there was a rag tied on her head. The Chief told them the man was their Medicine Man who was "taking care of your friend." They sure hoped this Medicine Man knew what he was doing. Tinker was looking pale as she laid on the Indian blanket. The girls couldn't wait to get Tinker back with them.

A Brave stuck his head in the funny house, "Chief, two of our Braves have their rifles and are pointing them at Billy. We need your help here for a minute."

The Chief came out to tell the ones who didn't go inside what was happening. Chief told his Braves "get rid of their rifles, Billy is our friend." The Braves walked back from where they came from.

"We have been treating 'Big Woman.' She is much better than when we brought her here. She was a mess. She had hit her head and has many bruises she received from her fall off her horse. Our Medicine Man helps."

The girls noticed that the Medicine Man had lit a small straw bundle and was waving the smoke all around Tinker. They thought, for sure, she would start coughing and choking. She had seen that on old TV shows, but never had seen it for real.

Tinker opened her eyes and smiled when she saw the girls. She told the girls the story about all that had happened to her and how scared she was. "I guess you heard that they renamed me 'Big Woman', but that doesn't bother me. I know I'm taller than most women, but I have been this way since I was a little girl."

"I thought you would be gone by now," Tinker told her friends.

Jas put her hand on Tinker's arm, "Tinker, we would never leave you. We love you, Tinker, and think of you as our cousin, and you may call us cousins. You are our honorary cousin. We are cousins forever.

When the girls looked at Tinker, they all noticed she had big tears in her eyes. The Chief came back in the house to tell Tinker she can leave when she is ready. He will get her horse for her. The Chief didn't say much, but they could see that he admired her stamina after he saw her injuries, and how she didn't cry or even complain.

An assemblage of Indian Braves was gathered to watch 'Big Woman.' There was much hooting and hollering at the Indian Camp for the strong woman that had been hurt. This made Tinker throw out a huge smile.

Billy told the others they needed to get to the cave before dark. They all agreed. They sure didn't want to ride around this country in the dark. Tinker was trying to get up, but when Jas saw her, she went over to help her up.

Jas smiled at Tinker, "Are you sure you will be able to ride back to the cave? Jas knew she needed to keep an eye out for her. She doesn't need to fall off her horse and fall on her head again.

Chapter Thirty

The ladies who went to the big Country Store, wanted to talk some more with Buzz and the Sheriff. Jayne told her husband she would cook dinner for everyone. She had already called Buxton and Buck along with Moonbeam. They liked Miss Jayne's home-cooked meals. They decided going over everything couldn't hurt anything.

They had to do something. The girls were becoming antsy to find their cousins. They wanted to talk again with the Fortune Teller called Moonbeam. They felt like she left out a few things. They had never talked with a Fortune Teller before, and they really didn't know how to take one. Most people around there were skeptical about talking to a Fortune Teller.

The girls and the others talked about the one from the past. Maybe, it is the two Indians. Another thing is some of the tracks could have been trampled making them look different. Most of the ones helping with this couldn't believe any of it.

The fire in the small fireplace was a given. Some caves are cold inside the cave. After searching around the small campfire, Buzz found a pack of matches and saw it had something written on it. It looked like a child's handwriting. It said, "From the Happy Slappy Saloon."

We wanted to make some kind of sense out of all this. We know they would need a fire to keep the chill off. Thank the Lord, for whoever left some matches not even one of the ladies had any matches.

"I don't know what it means when Moonbeam talked about the one from the past. I would think she was talking about the two Indians. They would still be Indians. Don't we have a few reservations around here?"

Moonbeam sat silently as she put her fingers to her temples.

"Moonbeam, is something wrong?" Jayne asked. She didn't like how Moonbeam was looking. It couldn't be something good.

"I just had a flash in my head. Someone is hurt," Moonbeam clarified.

"Do you know who it is? Can you see that?" Alaska asked.

"No, I only know that someone is hurt," Moonbeam wished she could see who it was, but it doesn't work that way. They knew everyone at the ranch had not been hurt, so it had to be one of the missing girls. This day was getting longer and longer. No one wanted any of them to be harmed, but they knew between Jayne and Nurse Olivia, they would be in good hands.

CHAPTER THIRTY-ONE

The Chiefs were back at the cave. They liked the cave much better than the town. The Chiefs started arguing almost the minute they stepped into the cave. It wasn't always something mean, but they were still talking faster than the others so they wouldn't be able to hear what they were saying.

They didn't really know where to go if they ever get back to Oklahoma. They have been gone for so long, they may not remember where they lived. One Chief lived in the Cherokee Reservation while the Choctaw went to where the Choctaws lived. They couldn't wait to return home. The ladies in the cave didn't understand why the Chiefs were there in the first place.

"We friends' long time. Sorry, your wife died," The Cherokee says.

"I will see you soon. Hate to say this, but I will miss our conversations. We have good ones." Choctaw Chief says.

"She talked much. Was good woman but talked too much."

"Why you Mother call you, 'Big Moon'?"

"She say: You have big butt."

"Why you Mother call you, 'He Who Wanders'?"

"She say I walk around at night."

"Why don't we go home this time? We can still see each other," 'Big Moon' said. "We can meet often."

"Good idea. Miss my family," 'He Who Wanders' thought it was time to go home, but the Choctaw and the Cherokee told each other they would see each other again and soon.

'He Who Wanders' looks at the girls. "Tell the other girls it was a pleasure to have met them. Same to you ladies, also. We leave now. Go home."

"We leave you now. 'Big Woman' should be able to ride her horse to the Cherokee Nation. They are good Indians and will not hurt you."

"We truly hope, the one who has a hurt head, will be well soon. The Medicine Man is good doctor."

"Good luck, Gentlemen," All the girls said as they watched the Indians go toward the door of the cave. They would miss their bantering with his friend when they leave.

Chapter Thirty-Two

The girls want to look at the cave again. Maybe someone will still be there. They would try anything to find the other girls. The girls that were left behind wondered if they were getting enough food and water or were they still together. They also wondered if they were hurt in some way. Not knowing exactly what may have happened to the girls. This was driving them all crazy, or crazier than normal. They were all praying for the best outcome. There had been many prayers for the missing girls ever since they found out they were missing.

Jayne told the girls she was coming with them. All the girls were ready as they put their guns in the holsters. This gave Jayne a great smile for the getting of their weapons. The other girls, who were lost, had their guns also, and they are missing. They all were missing the ladies and prayed they would see them soon.

Jayne knew Buzz wouldn't want us to go alone, so she found her phone out and called Buck. He answered immediately. She asked Buck if he would go with them to look around the cave one more time. Buck told Jayne was finished with his chores, and that he would be glad to go with them.

They were coming closer to the cave when Jayne looked at the girls and told them to stop.

"Everyone needs to be as quiet as they can when we get off our horses," Jayne was still smiling. She had a bag of sausage and biscuits. "If there are people in there, they must be hungry." Jayne was always thinking of others.

Grandee whispered to Olive, "Do you think there would be a snake in the cave?" Olive was sure hoping there was not a snake for Grandee's sake.

"Probably not, there is too much noise," Olive didn't know if that was so, or not, but she knew Grandee, and she was terrified of snakes, so she would make up something to pacify Grandee.

Olive told Grandee to stay behind her. That way Olive could kick the snake out of their way before Grandee even saw the snake. Callie thought she better whisper that because she didn't want Grandee to hear that there may very well be a snake in there.

The seven people walked slowly on tiptoes through the mouth of the cave. What they saw was certainly not a snake, and something they thought they would never see.

The girls stopped in their tracks when they saw two Indian Chiefs. They all were in awe at what they were looking at in this somewhat small cave. Jayne walked over to the Indians. The other girls and Buck admired Jayne's nerve. Buck still walked behind Jayne just in case of trouble. If something happened to her, Buzz would have a fit, so Buck will be very careful.

"Who are you?" Jayne asked. "Do you live here?"

"No live here," One of the Indians said. The Indians were just as confused as they were. No one seemed to know what to say. Jayne started the conversation, if it could be called a conversation.

"My name Jayne. I live around here. Do you both live in this cave?" Jayne didn't know how to talk to someone that says three-word sentences, but the others in the cave thought she was doing well.

"We are looking for the girl cousins. They came to explore the cave and now they are missing. Do you know if anyone besides the five girls and a small man were here? Do you know anything about this at all?"

"Sure," Cherokee Chief said as he smiled. "You talk too much."

"I tell you," The Choctaw Chief. "Pay him no attention, He not smart like me, I smart. He not." The ones who just got to the cave started chuckling.

"Excuse me. My friend delusional. I tell truth." The Cherokee Chief smiled at Jayne, "You pretty." Jayne didn't have the words, but it made her smile.

"Okay, tell us about what happened." Alaska was getting to become agitated. She liked people to spit out what they wanted to say, and not hesitate.

"We heard there was a small man in the cave. Can you tell us about him?" Jayne asked. "Do you know anything about the small man?"

"Of course, his real name is William H. Bonney."

"WOW! That's Billy the Kid," Houston said with a large smile. They all seemed to be in awe at the thoughts of Billy the Kid being in the very cave where they were standing.

"Where did everyone and their horses go?" Alaska asked, who was confused.

"It goes like this, a storm came and put their horses in the cave. The horses were agitated. We held on to our horses the best we could. "When the lightening flashed, we were standing in almost like a white thick cloud. When the cloud disappeared, we walked outside of another door to the cave. We couldn't find one for outside." The Cherokee explained.

"We saw an old town, so we went there. We were going to stay in the stable, but we didn't have ten bits. The Sheriff sent us to the Happy Slappy Saloon. The bartender gave the girls a dress, so they could dance for their stay in the stable. The Indian Chiefs were explaining the best they could. It was amazing the girls even got one bit after turning over a table that five men were sitting around making them all fall on the dirty floor, but when the girls put their tips together, they had just enough to stay the night in the stable.

The Sheriff came and wanted Billy. He said the bartender was dead, and Billy killed him. One of those girls told the Sheriff that Billy was with them all night. The Sheriff got mad and threw all of them in the Pokey. This story seemed to be what would be in a movie, but they didn't even know about movies back then.

They all got out of jail when the Sheriff saw the bartender, who wasn't dead at all. The last we saw them they were riding toward the cave. They were praying for a storm, so they went back to find her. They were not having too much trouble getting back to the cave.

The girls saw Billy riding up to the cave. He said he would help find the other girl. The happy group was debating where they should go east or west. He would do what he could. He didn't want to see anyone harmed. Billy was sure he didn't kill twenty-one men. He did have a heart, at times, but no one would believe it.

Chapter Thirty-Three

Jayne, the girls, and Buck went back to the cave. They were thinking there was something they were not seeing. The girls wanted to check things out in the cave. They were still thinking there must be some sort of door at the back of the cave. They didn't want to wait until Buzz got home to go with them. Jayne thought they should just be patient. She would feel better if Buzz was with her. Buck did a good job, but she would like for her husband to be there.

Jayne knew Buzz wouldn't want them to go without a man going with them, so Jayne went to the barn to talk to Buck. He knew Buzz was in meetings all day. Buck hesitated because he didn't want to make Buzz upset, but he finally said he would go. He figured Buzz wouldn't want the ladies to go by themselves.

Jayne, the girls, and Buck, made it back from the cave. Buzz had gotten back from his meetings. He was upset they went without him. Jayne told Buzz she got Buck to go with them.

The ladies told Buzz all about what they Indians said. He sat in awe as the girls talked. He had never heard such chatter as he was listening to right now. He didn't know what to say or do about all he was hearing.

"Did the Indian Chiefs say they were going back where they came from?" Buzz asked.

"He did a good job, and he finished his chores before we left," Jayne explained.

Buzz looked at his wife, "It's okay. I'm glad Buck was able to go with you and the girls."

"The Indians told us a lot because they were with the girls the whole time." They don't speak very many words at one time, but we did learn some things you may not believe.

"That was nice of the Indians to help with the girls. If I see them, I will thank them myself," Buzz smiled at the ladies. He couldn't believe the girls went inside the cave and talked to two Indian Chiefs. He knew Jayne liked talking to new people, but he couldn't let her go up to the Indians and start a conversation.

The girls at the house were missing Jas, Callie, Phoenix, Tinker, and Olivia. They will give them big hugs as soon as they find them and find them, they will. They wouldn't have it any other way. They sure hope the others will be found soon. They didn't like it when the girls were separated.

Buzz says, "Let's all go to bed and try for a good night's sleep. I want to go to the cave tomorrow. I need to check these Indians out, or maybe he would need to check the inside of the cave before letting other people go inside it. I want to go to the cave tomorrow. I want to talk to the Chiefs."

"Good idea, Buzz." Buxton was there and decided he would go with them. He didn't want to be left out, "besides if there is trouble, we may be needed in there." The girls, who were not missing, said they would go too. They thought this was a great opportunity to learn new things.

The girls got up and walked to the bunkhouse. They looked at the main house and noticed all the lights were off. Before they went to their bunkhouse, they saw the Indians being taken to the barn, with Jayne taking them blankets. They thought Jayne and Buzz were nice to let the Indians stay in their barn.

Chapter Thirty-Four

Everyone went to the back patio for a good breakfast. After eating, they all headed out for the cave. Buzz wanted to talk to the Indians. He wondered why Jayne walked right up to the Indians and started a conversation. He was curious about what was happening in there. Jayne will talk to anyone. Buzz was curious about what was happening in there.

"I wanted to say, 'thank you' for looking after the girls," Buzz says to the Indian Chiefs.

"We watch them. No problem," 'Big Moon' said." It was beginning to be chilly in the cave, so Phoenix started a campfire. It was dark and the fire felt good.

"I would like to talk to the Indians," Buzz says to the others.

Jas told Buzz she saw them outside taking a walk. "I'll wait for a while," Buzz said.

Jayne told Buzz she listened to the weather report today and there will be a brewing storm tonight. Buzz says he wanted to get the Indians and the others who were with them because he wanted them out of the storm.

"There will be a raging storm tonight. Buzz says he wanted to get the Indians and the others who were with them out of the storm."

"Did y'all have fun at the store?" Buxton asked with a huge smile.

"Yeah, it was a great trip." They all agreed.

Houston smiled as she told the cave girls that they purchased all a T-shirt from Oklahoma. Jas says they will pay whoever paid for the shirts. They knew Jas would agree, and they would all pay Houston back later.

"Jayne, we need to round up our new guests before this weather gets closer to us.

After they arrived at Buzz and Jayne's house, they saw Buzz and Buxton going toward the barn. Jayne had her arms full of a heap of blankets for the Indians.

They thought it was so nice of them to help the Indians and let them stay here in their barn. Jayne told them all that the report said this was going to be a bad one.

CHAPTER THIRTY-FIVE

Jayne, Buzz, and girls went to tell the Indians they are going to our house to get you out of the storm. The Indians were smiling like circus clowns. They had never been in white man's house before. Jayne invited them in the house and explained where they would be sleeping. The Indians told her to not make a fuss over them. They had never slept in a barn before. They thought it may be nice. They didn't want to make a mess for Miss Jayne to clean up.

"What about other girls?" 'Big Moon' asked. Buzz thought it was nice that they wanted to take care of the girls. They almost thought the Indians liked the girls. Buzz thought it might be a good thing to have the Indians to help take care of others.

They will need a bad storm to put them back in the cave. They all wondered how they knew about the lightning. This was confusing to the others. Perhaps, they have done this many times.

Then Buxton smiled and glanced around the room. "Do we know anything about Billy?"

"The Indians said Billy went with the other girls to find Tinker. She had been hurt," 'He Who Wanders' said. He worried about the girls.

'He Who Wanders' said, "Indian don't know where Billy went after helping with the hurt girl."

"We see Billy come to cave, but he left with girls to search for 'Big Woman.' Couldn't find her."

"Maybe they find her."

Lots of animals and snakes around the area. There is also a Creek Nation somewhere out there. "Those Indians stupid," says the laughing girls, but they stopped when they had time to think about it all.

"We were listening when Billy came up on his horse. The girls told him where they were going, and he said he would go with them. He came back to take care of the ladies. He was worried about them." That made the ladies smile. They were sure they would never forget about Billy the Kid, or the two Indian Chiefs who were a touch crazy, but thoughtful at the same time.

'He Who Wanders' was shaking his head like he didn't know what to do next. "Don't know anything." Cherokee smiled.

The Indians began telling the others exactly what happened and why they were gone. "It's coming up a storm. We tell how it works." Everyone stopped and listened to hear what the Chief has to say.

"When a large streak of lightening finally struck bad, you go through a white thick cloud. Then we went outside and there was the Old Western Town. I don't know why they call it Old. It has been there for many moons. So, girls need strong lightening to strike to get them back in the cave. Then they can come here."

"After we arrive in the town, we sure needed a place to stay, and Billy got us the stable to stay and put up our horses. The girls didn't have ten bits, so they made the girls go to the bartender in town, and he gave them pretty dresses. Said they could dance with some of the men, and they will get tip. They finally got what they needed so we could all stay in the stable."

"The next day they came to take Billy and put him in jail for killing the bartender. The girls knew the bartender wasn't dead, because he was still working in the Happy Slappy Saloon. The Sheriff put us in jail too. He was a little short man that wore a cowboy hat that was bigger than him," Cherokee Chief explained it all, so the others wouldn't think anything bad about the girls.

CHAPTER THIRTY-SIX

Buxton stayed the night in the house with Buzz and Jayne. Buxton and Buck went to the Feed and Seed store to pick up some things for the horses. Buck was looking to see if they had everything on the list.

While walking around, he saw a lovely lady with long black hair and dark blue eyes. She had on the normal clothing for the times. Her long dress looked to be something a Queen would wear. Buxton was sure she wasn't a Queen, but she sure was pretty. She had a bridle in her hands. She turned around and introduced herself to Buxton, but she was staring straight at Buxton. She said her name was Amy Moss.

Buxton never thought he would meet a girl in a Feed Store. He walked over where she was standing and asked if he wanted to know if he would have a cup of coffee with her at the coffee shop next door. She smiled and said, "That would be wonderful. Thank you."

Buck heard their conversation and would be teasing Buxton about it by now if the girl wasn't still standing there. He figured he would get his time for teasing Buxton another day.

"Great." Buxton was jumpy outside his body. He didn't want to ruin this chance. She was much too pretty for him, but he will give it a try. She was not only pretty, but she was a good person.

Buxton knew his brother was wondering if he would find anyone else. His wife left him about a year ago without a word. She didn't call at all. He thought it was time to go forward with his life. No one would blame him for seeing a lovely girl.

CHAPTER THIRTY-SEVEN

The girls and Billy got back to the cave with Tinker riding slowly on her horse. Billy noticed the ladies were going slowly so Tinker wouldn't be alone. They knew they needed to watch her due to her head injury.

Tinker laughed along with the others when someone said something funny. She loved the cousins for not leaving her out in the wild. It made her cry when the girls said she will be their honorary cousin. She didn't know how she had been so blessed, but she intended to thank the Lord in her nightly prayers.

The ladies and Billy saw the cave first. They all searched for the special door that was supposed to get them to the back of the cave.

They all heard the loud sound of the storm that was coming closer every minute. They hurried and got their horses to the front. They all waited while holding their breaths for that strike of lightning.

They all brought their horses with them so they wouldn't be spooked by the storm when it came. They kept a good grip on the reins so they wouldn't try to run away. After all, the horses belonged to Buzz and Jayne, so they would take good care of them.

They noticed that Billy and his horse was beside them in the cave. Jas stayed close to Tinker because she wasn't sure that Tinker was better. Jas would keep an eye on her anyway. Jas knew Tinker was a strong woman, but she still would worry about her.

Billy and the ladies heard the awful sound of a raging storm. They hurried to get their horses to the cave. They hurried to get their horses to the front. Everyone waited for that strike of the bright light.

Chapter Thirty-Eight

All the ones at the home of Buzz and Jayne noticed the clouds were beginning to darken and looking like it may rain any minute. They heard the thunder and the strikes of lightning. It was a touch scary, but if what the Indians said was true, it could mean the other ladies would be back soon.

Jayne looked at her guests and smiled. "You know, I was thinking this would be a good time for the ones missing to be back in the cave. I just feel it in my bones."

"I sure hope you are right. We may see them riding up at your barn any minute, now." Jas always tried to keep a positive attitude about everything. They didn't know what they would do without Jas. She keeps everyone on the right track.

"I was praying they were all okay. You never know about these storms. They are probably hungry and in need of water," Grandee said with a frown. "They would also want to have a nice long hot shower."

Buxton glanced at the others in the house, "I think Grandee is right. They will, most likely, want food. They need to have food after this wild adventure.

"You're right, Buxton. Buzz and I have been smoking some BBQ all day. It may be ready shortly." Everyone that were at the house could smell the aroma of the BBQ. Everyone loved their BBQ.

Olive spoke, "I will help Jayne in the kitchen." Olive was always ready to help anyone, so she would be happy to help Jayne in the kitchen. She liked helping in the kitchen, and Jayne loved having these spirited girls in there. Jayne liked having them in the kitchen singing and dancing while they helped Jayne.

Grandee and Houston jumped up and said they would help Jayne, also. The ladies sauntered into the kitchen while laughing. They were being hopeful they would see the other cousins. Jayne liked having them in the kitchen singing and dancing while they helped her.

"Everyone, listen. Do you hear what I hear?" Buzz smiled.

"I don't hear anything," Alaska said. She tucked her hair behind her ears so she could hear better what was going on.

Buzz looked at the people in his barn and stopped with a huge smile and told everyone to be quiet.

"Exactly. The rain has stopped, and Buzz told everyone to be quiet and listen.

Jayne was standing at the kitchen staring out the window as she watched who was riding up to the barn. She saw the girls coming on their horses. She watched to see who was riding up to the barn, and she dropped what she was doing as she ran to the barn.

"Everyone, come quickly. Run to the barn," Jayne could hardly get her breath as she watched the missing girls dismount their horses.

They all ran to the barn to see how everything was with them. Some were wet from the storm while others were shaking the rain from their coats.

Jayne and the other ladies ran toward the wet girls, and one Billy the Kid. There were huge hugs as they all laughed at being back at Buzz and Jayne's house.

Jayne showed the girls where they could get out of their wet clothes. She noticed a few of them were shaking. Grandee was right. They will need a quick hot shower. Jayne had towels she had put in the microwave, so they would be warm for the girls. The ladies thought Jayne was a very thoughtful lady.

Buzz looked at the wet young man the girls brought back from the cave. He was wet, and they didn't think they had ever seen him before.

Buzz went over to the young man and shook his hand. "My name is Buzz and this is my ranch. We are glad to have you. If you want to, you are welcome to take a hot shower.

Billy held out his hand to Buzz's hand so he could introduce himself. "My name is William H. Bonney, but everyone calls me Billy.

Jayne almost fainted, but she got over it.

CHAPTER THIRTY-NINE

They all saw the Indian Chiefs leave with the girls, Buzz, and Jayne.

Buzz ran to stop them from leaving. "Don't go yet," Buzz told the ones who were leaving. Buzz wanted them to all stay. They need food.

Jayne says we need to have a party tonight. Buzz agreed to the party and a barn dance.

The Indian Chief walks over to Buzz. "You have Fire Water tonight. It makes people either funny or sad."

"No, Fire Water. I promise," Buzz says with a large smile.

The wet girls finally made it to the barn. Everyone was dancing and having a good time. The band was great. Buzz was lucky to get them on such short notice. The band started a fast song. Billy walked over to Jayne and took Jayne's hand and said, "Ma'am, may I have this dance?"

Billy started doing something close to an Irish Jig. He told Jayne he would teach her the Jig.

Next, Billy went up to Jas who was sitting and smiling. Billy took her hand and told Jas she was the prettiest girl in the barn, and he would be right proud to have her dance with him. The girls had been talking about Buxton and that he needed a girl of his own. They thought it was awful about his wife leaving him. He was so handsome.

The girls couldn't believe what they saw coming in the double doors of the big red barn. The girls were giggling. They had just finished their conversation on how Buxton needs a girlfriend to go out and eat and go to movies, or wherever they want to go. We don't want him to be lonely. Now, here he comes with a lovely lady on his arm. The girls wanted to jump up and down but didn't want to see Buxton sad.

Jayne and Buzz went over to Buxton to tell his brother to introduce the lady. Jayne couldn't wait to hear all about Buxton's new girl. She thought it was about time he found a girlfriend. Buzz loved his brother and wanted him to be happy.

"Buxton, are you going to introduce us to your lady?" Buzz smiled at the look on Buxton's face. Yep, he was smitten.

"I'm sorry, this lovely is Amy Moss. Amy, this is my brother, Buzz, and my lovely sister-in-law is Jayne.

"Buxton, you should have told us about Amy," Jayne says.

Amy looks at Buzz and Jayne, "That would be my fault. We just met yesterday, but I guess we kind of hit it off as we had coffee together yesterday. We first met in the Feed and Seed Store where I was getting a new bridle."

"We are so happy to meet you. Go get some BBQ Buxton and I made. Then, there is dancing."

Jayne and Buzz liked Buxton's new girl from the first they saw and heard her talk.

"Thanks for having me," Amy says with a sweet smile. Jayne thought this one was a keeper.

Chapter Forty

Jayne and Buzz let Billy in the guest room. They were excited to have Billy in the house. He didn't seem like he was a mean person. Billy, Jayne, and Buzz stayed in the living room talking to Billy. He told his host and Hostess that Jas has been researching Billy. He told them he hadn't done some of the things Jas told him about.

"If I killed anyone, it was in self-defense. I wouldn't do anything to anyone on your ranch. I appreciate you letting me stay in your spare room. I can get up early in the morning and leave.

"Tell the girls I said goodbye. I should have told them before they went to bed. I want to try my best to be a better person. It may be hard because I have run with some mean men, but I'm pretty sure I will be able to do better. Maybe if I get in with a bad crowd, I should think of these ladies because he wouldn't want to disappoint them."

Buzz looked around the room, "We really should get a good night's sleep."

"Billy don't leave before breakfast in the morning. I usually make a big breakfast, and you may not get another home-cooked meal for a while.

"Okay, Ma'am. I would like that. My Mama always made a big breakfast. I sure do miss my Mama."

"Billy, do you have enough cover on your bed?" Billy says thank you for the thought, but he will do just fine. He didn't want to make more work for Miss Jayne. "I don't want to be a bother, Ma'am."

Everyone said their good nights and went to bed. Billy laid down on a bed he thought felt like sleeping on pillows. He also thought the sheets smelled great.

The morning was full of bright sunshine making everyone feel much better. Everybody ate a huge breakfast with all the new friends.

"Billy, where will you be headed?" Buzz asked. He was still curious about Billy.

"I think I will go back to the Creek Indians. I promised them I would let them know how Tinker was doing." Billy stated. "They are not mean Indians unless someone hurts one of their people. I have known them for quite a while. They took a bullet out of my back one time."

"Be careful out there, Billy," Buzz said that he would. He got up to go to the barn to saddle his horse.

He hugged all the girls and told them he would be doing better now. They were all good influences on him. He promised the girls he would try his best to do better. He also promised them that he would visit his Mama.

The girls wanted to ride along with Billy for a while to make sure he gets to where he is going. They had been riding for an hour before they heard gunfire. All the ladies pulled their pistols out to help, if they could.

Billy told the girls to get behind the big rocks and stay down. "I don't want anything to happen to you nice ladies."

Outlaws fire at Billy. Phoenix stood up from her rock. She aimed her pistol toward the man that was talking to Billy. Phoenix shot the man on his gun arm. She usually hits what she is aiming at. The man looked at Phoenix like he could kill her. In his time, ladies didn't wear britches. The man aimed his gun at Phoenix and shot missing Phoenix by an inch.

"What's wrong, Billy, you need to get women to protect you?"

"Shut up, Luke. These are my friends. You know better than to shoot women."

"I can't wait until you get ready to tell me what this is all about," The man with a gun says.

"Luke, I'm not going to ride with you anymore," Billy said to the man.

"You a chicken, Billy?"

"You know me better than that." Billy explained. If Phoenix hadn't shot him, he would have done it himself. He is a bad man.

"I made up my mind when you shot that little girl last week. She was the same age as my sister. It wasn't necessary to shoot her. What did you think she was going to do to you?" Billy was still upset about the little girl.

Billy took a shot on his shoulder. Jas made her way to where Billy was sitting and bleeding.

"Jas, what do we do now?" Billy asked.

"We need to get Billy back to Buzz's house. He needs some ointment and a bandage, so he won't get infected." Jas wanted to make sure Billy got the treatment he needed.

"Billy, hold on. Don't move too much." Jas had a scarf and used the scarf to press his shoulder with the scarf to help the blood flowing down his arm. The others thought Jas knew what she was doing.

"Y'all Listen, we can't let Billy die because we can't change history."

It took a while and three stout ladies to put Billy on the back of his horse. They found out that the outlaws took off. "They are gone. Now, we ride for Buzz and Jayne's house." Some of the girls rode back to tell Buzz and Jayne what had happened. When the girls brought Billy back, he saw that Jayne had already had bandages ready and a nice clean bed.

CHAPTER FORTY-ONE

After finally pushing Billy on his horse, the girls were taking him to Jayne. She would know what to do, along with Olivia, who was a nurse. Olivia stayed with Jayne while Houston and Callie went to help in the kitchen. Everyone was agitated over all that has happened in the last few days.

Before they arrived at the house, Jas noticed that Billy was barely staying in the saddle. She jumped off her horse and hopped on the back of Billy's saddle and took the reins so he couldn't fall off on the hard ground. The girls, who were with Billy, were somewhat worried they wouldn't have him back at the ranch in time.

"Phoenix, can you grab the reins on my horse, so she won't run away?" Phoenix rode and went to get Jas's horse.

"Sure," Phoenix reached those reins without getting off her horse making the others stared in wonder with mouth's wide open at what Phoenix did. They knew she was good around horses, but they had no idea she could do tricks.

While Phoenix was doing her circus act, Olive was on the phone talking to Jayne. Jayne started chuckling as she watched Phoenix do her thing.

"I called Jayne. She and Olivia will get things ready to see what they can do to help Billy." Everyone was going to do whatever they needed to do. They knew Billy couldn't die now.

The girls made it back to Jayne and Olivia. Buxton and Buck met them to help get Billy off the horse and into the house. That's when Jayne told them where to put him. They noticed Billy was beginning to bleed again. Jayne and Olivia went to work.

"His wound is bleeding more, and he has a high fever. We need to get him to a hospital," Olivia says in her best nurse voice. Olivia knew just what to do. She would go with them for the trip to the hospital.

"He may have a heart attack if we put him in an ambulance with a siren blaring. We need to remember he has never seen all that he would be seeing," Alaska says. The others agreed with Alaska.

Buzz and Buck put one of the mattresses in the bed of Buzz's Dooley to take him to the hospital. Buzz sat on the mattress with Billy, while Buxton drove the truck.

Billy started talking when they put him in the truck. "I am sorry for some of the things I have done. I want to be more like the girls. They are so nice and kind." Buzz told Billy to be calm and try not to talk. We will take care of you.

"Billy, you can be the way you want to be," Olive says with a bright sweet smile. "We all know you can do it, man."

Everyone went to the hospital. She was thinking she was still hurting some herself. Tinker didn't want to be in the way, but she wanted to go with them and see how Billy does.

The doctor came in and ask Billy what his name was. The others were holding their breath at what Billy might say. They didn't want to shock anyone.

He told the doctor his name was William Corn, but everyone just calls him Billy. He was afraid to let anyone here in this white place that has an awful smell, to know his real name.

"Whoever put the rag on his wound when it first was made had saved his life," The doctor was amazed that Billy was still alive.

Buzz didn't know exactly what to say how Billy was shot because it would require the hospital calling the police, but Buzz knew the Sheriff well, so he would take care of it. Thank goodness for his friendship with the Sheriff. People may not take this well if they knew.

"That would have been Jas who put the rag on Billy," Grandee said with a large smile. "She is always willing to help."

The doctor came back to where everyone was sitting. "I noticed that I had never seen a bullet like that before," he told them they could take Billy home. "Keep the wound clean. I will send some things home with you. He should be good to go in another week, or whenever he feels like it."

"We have a nurse at my house helping Jayne. That should make things a bit better." Buzz explained. "I'm sure they will take care of him."

"That's great. I know Jayne will take good care of this young man. I have complete confidence in her." The doctor looked at all who were in the white smelly room.

"I have some help coming to get him on a stretcher to help put him wherever it is you brought him in.

Buzz told the doctor he brought him in the back of his Dooley. The doctor just shook his head the same way he shook it when he saw the bullet he took out of this kid.

Buzz never seems to make me smile when he brings in some of the things he has had to treat. Buzz brought in a sick pig one time.

The doctor had a hunch, so he went in his office and started laughing when he looked at the old picture when he saw what he had been looking for. He found a picture of Billy the Kid on the internet.

Chapter Forty-Two

The doctor, who realized who the man was, knew who Buzz had brought in the ER. He would talk about that with Buzz another time and place. The doctor started chuckling as he went to his office. He still couldn't believe he treated the wounds of the real Billy the Kid.

Buzz thought of something. Tinker was in the waiting room with the other girls and Jayne. Buzz went to the waiting room and got Tinker and took her to see the same doctor that had treated Billy.

"Hey, Doc, we sort of have another patient for you to see. She was bucked off her horse and she fell a long way into a huge hole. The Creeks found her and took care of her, but I thought she may need some modern medicine.

"She probably would like some more up-to-date medicine." Since Tinker had been in a dirty hole and had a lot of bruises. Her head was checked to see if it had gotten better. He said her head seemed to be doing okay. "I'll give her something in case she starts having more headaches." Tinker looked at them confused.

Tinker looked at the doctor. "Am I okay?"

"Yes, for what you have been through, you are in great health. I'm going to give you an antibiotic just in case. You were in a dirty hole with a few injuries. You are lucky there wasn't a big rattlesnake in that hole with you, little lady.

"Thanks for calling me little. I don't get that much." Tinker smiled at the tall handsome doctor.

"Doctor, please tell me you will not get a bundle of sage and hover the smoke all over my body. That is what the Indians did to me. They also put a rag over my head which wasn't very clean."

"I think we can do better than that. Take the antibiotic like it says to do, and you should be good to go," The Doctor explained.

"It sure was nice to meet you, Miss Tinker. Are all these girls I saw in the waiting room kin to you?" Tinker assured him they were.

"Buzz has brought me some rare patients, but I help them when I can. He brought me a calf one night when everyone was gone. I gave the calf a shot and sent him home."

The doctor had Tinker laughing which she liked to do. "Those girls are cousins, but I'm an honorary cousin. They have been the best friends a girl could have."

The doctor put his head close to Tinker's and gave her a big ole slobbery kiss that almost made her faint. She knew she would be smiling for the rest of the night.

Tinker knew she would tell the others, and would most likely, wouldn't sleep a lick all night long. When she went in the waiting room with a gigantic smile that covered her whole face, the girls began wondering what had happened to Tinker. Tinker told them, and they all started laughing. "You go, girl."

Tinker was laughing with them. She was so happy right now she could fly up in the sky. She didn't regret one single moment of her vacation at the ranch of Buzz and Jayne.

She missed all the vacations when she never went anywhere except her little cabin in Texas. When she went to her first vacation, she thought of all the years she could have been enjoying traveling and meeting new people. Now, that she was an honorary cousin to the girls, she would be doing more things.

Chapter Forty-Three

All the cousins were overjoyed to finally being together with each other. They knew they would never have another adventure like this one ever again. They always talk about all the adventures they had before they even knew me. I try my best to keep them safe and out of trouble.

They thought they had been blessed to have healthy bodies that lets them be able to do the things that they do.

They also were jumping with joy that Jayne will be able to go on an adventure with the cousins next summer. They haven't decided exactly where they would go, but between all the ladies, they always find a great place, and they are never disappointed.

They know they are getting a little older, and they want to do things before they may not be as healthy. A couple of the ladies are a few years older than the others.

They really thought they would love to stay at Buzz and Jayne's ranch, but they didn't want to be a burden. They really didn't know how Jayne can do all that she does.

The girls were glad they could help her with her chores. Buzz, Buxton, Buck, and everyone else on the ranch were great people.

Aside from some of the ladies coming up missing, they still had a great time. They still couldn't believe seeing

Billy the Kid, and they still would like to know why the Indian Chiefs were in the cave. At times, the girls got a good chuckle from their small conversations.

Jayne and Buzz tried to get the cousins to stay a while longer, but a couple of the cousins had to get back to work. A few of them do volunteer work. They did their vacations once a year so they can save up some money during the year.

Most of the husbands always ask their wives when they return, "What did you ladies do this time?"

Epilogue

There were much mind-boggling activities around Buzz and Jayne's ranch this fine sunny morning. Buxton came to eat breakfast. The visiting ladies were leaving in a couple hours. Buzz, Jayne, Buxton, and Buck would miss the girls when they left for their homes.

The Indian Chiefs left after a hardy breakfast. Buzz was thinking they had never seen people eat so much. It was like they had never eaten that much at one time before.

Before Billy left, he was sitting with the Indians in deep conversation with the Chiefs. Billy got sort of attached to the Chiefs. He would miss them arguing with each other. They kept him entertained. The Chiefs went home after everyone said good-bye. Billy was grateful Olivia put a clean bandage on his wound before he left. They all watched as one Chief went left while the other one went to the right.

The lady cousins were packing and made a trip to the barn to see the horses they had been riding during this trip. They had made new friends and one of the friends they made, they knew they would never see again. No way they would see Billy the Kid, but they will have memories of their time with him. Every time they see an old Western on TV that has Billy the Kid in it, they will always remember their memories and what he was like in real life.

Their time in Oklahoma was coming to an end, but their trip can only be described as magnificent.

Buzz, Jayne and Buxton were on the porch waiting to hug the ladies before they go back home. They sure would miss those ladies. They were all kind and nice.

The girls were laughing and having fun about this trip. Even with some of the girls being lost, they still called it a fantastic trip. Buck figured the mold was broken with these women. There will never be others that can top these ladies.

They walked to the front porch where their host and hostess were sitting. Everyone got up and the hugging began. Everyone was talking and laughing as they talked about the fun adventure they had.

The ladies piled in Callie's red van with the white stripe wondering if they would ever have another trip this exciting again. They were sure to have some adventures no matter where they go on vacation next.

Other Books Written by
Sherry Moss Walraven

A Lesson Long Ago
Mountain Adventure
Wild Ride at the Dude Ranch
Outdoor Vacation with a Twist
Haunted Holiday
A Revolutionary Adventure
A Flower for a Ranch
Once in a Lifetime
Midnight Terror
It Happened One Spooky Night in October
Bye Bye Dear Lily
Intriguing Escapade at Swim Camp
You Can't Catch Me
Midnight Struggle
Oklahoma Trail Ride
The Sistas of Hooverville County

www.ingramcontent.com/pod-product-compliance
Lightning Source LLC
LaVergne TN
LVHW050024080526
838202LV00069B/6903